DROUGHT

Drought

RONALD FRASER

VERSO
London • New York

First published by Verso 2015
© Estate of Ronald Fraser 2015

1 3 5 7 9 10 8 6 4 2

Verso
UK: 6 Meard Street, London W1F 0EG
US: 20 Jay Street, Suite 1010, Brooklyn, NY 11201
www.versobooks.com

Verso is the imprint of New Left Books

ISBN-13: 978-1-78168-897-7 (PB)
eISBN-13: 978-1-78168-898-4 (US)
eISBN-13: 978-1-78168-899-1 (UK)

British Library Cataloguing in Publication Data
A catalogue record for this book is available from the British Library

Library of Congress Cataloging-in-Publication Data

Fraser, Ronald, 1930–2012.
Drought : a novel / Ronald Fraser.
    pages cm
  ISBN 978-1-78168-897-7 (hardback) – ISBN 978-1-
78168-898-4 (ebk)
1. British – Spain – Fiction. 2. Spain – History – Civil
War, 1936–1939 – Fiction. 3. Spain – History –
1939–1975 – Fiction. I. Title.
 PR6106.R45446D86 2015
 823'.92–dc23

                    2015006190

Typeset in Fournier by MJ & N Gavan, Truro, Cornwall
Printed in the US by Maple Press

Drought

A Note in Time

I visited Benalamar this year, in memory of my friend and colleague John Black. In its small way, the trip was a tribute to the influence he had on my life; and (though I have only recently discovered it) a recognition of the influence Benalamar had on his.

I'd read – who hasn't? – that the surrounding countryside had become one of the sought-after residential tourist areas in this part of Spain. Even so, I was surprised. Driving up from Torre del Mar on the coast, I barely recognized John's description of the countryside as it was thirty years ago. Large houses hidden by walls and eucalyptus, svelte lawns and swimming pools rapidly glimpsed, an eighteen-hole golf course had turned it into something more like a country club estate. Evidently, John's fears (and the dreams of his contemporary, Bob, a London property developer) had come true.

Consulting the hand-drawn map that John had left with the manuscript, I looked for Miguel's farmstead and found it, I think: a foreigner's low-slung ranch-house stood on the terraces where Miguel's crops had shrivelled in that summer of drought. The cottage was gone, perhaps never rebuilt.

Round a corner the village suddenly appeared, cubes of white and red-brown tiles, cascading down its hill and I recognized it instantly from what I had read. The square, its bare earth tiled over, appeared as I'd imagined, the fountain now splashing water from its five spouts. Now there were no men standing against the walls waiting for work. In their place a swarm of tourists followed a guide. I discovered John's house; it had been turned into a souvenir shop. Bob's, if I located it correctly, was a tourist restaurant. My wife and children would gladly have spent the rest of the holiday in the new four-star hotel with swimming pool, sauna, tennis courts on the outskirts of the village. They fell in love with Benalamar. But I refused to stay more than one night, a night I spent re-reading John's script.

We both knew he was dying, but we seldom referred to it. He wanted to continue working until the end, to 'die in harness' as he once said, and I admired his courage. There was, therefore, no sense of finality when one day he came into my office and said he'd be grateful if I could keep this folder for him. He handed it to me, and I saw it contained a typescript with many emendations in his small handwriting. 'Of course,' I said. And as an afterthought: 'Have you started writing again?' He laughed. 'No, it's an old thing I found the other day. My flat is overflowing with scripts as it is.'

I put the folder in a drawer and, to my shame, forgot about it. I was heavily engaged at the time in negotiations with the American conglomerate that was proposing to buy out our publishing firm; and it was only some months later, after John's death at the early age of fifty-seven, that I remembered it. I was sorting through his personal papers in the office for his nephew and executor, and the script came to mind. Before handing it over I took it home to read.

John was my oldest friend; we first met on a London newspaper over thirty years ago, and on his return from Spain I helped to get him a job at the publishers where I had found work. Despite our closeness, he rarely, if ever, spoke of his time in Benalamar where he had gone to recuperate from a mysterious illness. The script was all the more interesting when I discovered that it concerned his experiences there.

Reading it, I understood why he preferred not to talk of those times: his involvement in the suicide of the sharecropper, Miguel, was a bitter moment and I think left deep scars, deeper perhaps than he deserved to bear. I also understood why he came to consider *indifference* (to society, to others) a cardinal sin and became a committed socialist. The roots lay in that summer in Benalamar.

Of almost as great fascination to me was the picture he drew of a village living in a pre-modern era; or perhaps more accurately, of Andalusian rural life on the cusp of – and resisting – modernization. A modernization which, as I think he only partly foresaw, was a new form of colonization: mass tourism. It was hard to believe that the events he witnessed, and to some extent participated in, should have happened only thirty years ago.

He was then twenty-seven, and his script bears the marks of his youth. I recognize myself in much of what he writes: we were a great deal more ingenuous (and also more deferential) than the young of today. There have been many welcome changes since then. A young man today would surely not be content to attempt a straightforward reconstruction of another's life, as John tried to do with Miguel: he would have Lacan at his elbow; or Paul Auster looking over his shoulder. There would be a contemporaneous sense of the uncertainties of the age. But (and I feel the need to insist) John's narrative, in its endeavour to comprehend and explain Miguel's life, would have struck his own contemporaries as a familiar enterprise rooted in a Sartrean optimism that the unknown, the uncertain can be explained (although in this case at an imaginary level).

It is not my place to comment further; I am surely not my friend's best judge. But there is one part of the story that is history, and its impact, I fear, may be insufficiently understood by a new generation of readers from John's brief comments. I'm referring to the Anglo-French invasion of Egypt, in collusion with Israel, in 1956 after Nasser, the Egyptian leader, nationalized the Suez Canal. Though Britain was still involved in colonial wars, it was the first outright British invasion of a sovereign state since the end of the second world war. In that period of decolonization, Britain had suddenly returned – in a move planned secretly and almost alone by Eden, the Tory prime minister, who believed Nasser was another Hitler – to its imperial, gunboat past.

For once, the Labour Party stood firm in opposition, and found many people like John and me, unquantifiable liberals, supporting it. John, who was then a junior leader writer on the paper, was thrust into writing editorials supporting the invasion – having to deputize for his senior, who was ill – and his reaction was one of impotent rage. My anger led me to resign. It was the only time I can recall that we reacted in very different ways. Suez, and the almost contemporaneous crushing of the Hungarian uprising by Khrushchev, the Soviet leader who only three years before had uttered his (partial) indictment of Stalin's excesses, was the sharp awakening for many of my generation, as the Vietnam war in the late sixties was for a future generation. West and East seemed equally contemptible in our eyes.

The following morning, helped by an amiable town hall official who spoke excellent English, I succeeded in locating Dolores. She is seventy now and lives in the house where she lived thirty years ago. It took her a moment to recall John's name. But then it returned:

'Ah, Sr John! Yes! And you are his friend!' She greeted me

warmly. 'How is he? He wouldn't recognize the village today.' Everything was so much better now, she went on expansively, as she showed me round her house and its renovated interior. Among the many other things – three-piece suite and TV set in the small downstairs room – the house had running water from the village mains.

'And now everyone has work building, the land is barely farmed any more, there's no need to irrigate …' The return of democracy after Franco's death had brought a socialist town hall which was working for the people. And tourism was thriving.

I continued to put off the moment I knew had to come and asked about some of the people who figured in John's time here: the señorita, María Burgos, whose actions were largely responsible for what happened that summer, died fifteen years ago. Her heirs sold all her land, including El Mayorazgo, to foreigners. Ana married a mechanic and lived on the coast. Dolores herself had worked as a cook in one of the new foreigners' homes until she retired. No one had heard of Bob for years; he'd built a few houses and one day disappeared.

When I told her about John she threw up her hands and tears came to her eyes. 'So young, so young!' Sitting down, she dabbed at her cheeks. Had it been the old illness? No, I said, he'd recovered from that. 'Ay! Poor man. It's the best who go first.'

She recalled some of her memories and I was touched by her evident affection for him. I told her all that there was to tell of John's life after she'd known him, and we left each other deeply moved.

I walked through the village until I came to where John's map indicated a threshing floor and the start of the track down to El Mayorazgo. I found myself standing on the edge of a car park searching for a faint trace between new houses; and far down, looking for a landmark, I found what I took to be the dam on which Bob had gambled everything, a gash in the ravine, abandoned and empty, it seemed. A jagged line of rock showed where, probably, it had been repaired after the final catastrophe. Above it, the houses he had evidently built as part of his development were small, almost insignificant beside the latest accretions. Like many a pioneer, he seemed not to have benefited from his dreams; he had been before his time and seemed to have vanished in time like so much else.

Then I thought I could just make out a part of the track cutting its way down the side of the rock to the watercourse and through the hills to El Mayorazgo. Here John had so often stood before beginning the steep walk down; or turned round, after the long climb back, to look at the rounded hills below. Amidst the tourist cars, I tried to imagine myself in his place at that moment when his story begins.

David Symmons
London, 1989

I. Words

1

And then, on the mule track far below, the coffin appeared.

'Ay! They're bringing him up now.'

Borne on indistinguishable shoulders, the coffin was no more than a wavering smudge as it emerged into the sunlight on this side of the hills. Behind it a few small figures walked.

'They've stopped, they're changing shoulders now.'

The foreigner stared. In the shade of the rock, where the cortege had halted, he saw only an uncertain movement, a fusion of figures. Sweat condensed on his back.

'There's the carob tree, señor, by the watercourse.' Gnarled fingers stabbed down towards the earth. 'That's where they found him.'

'I know.'

He turned his back on the old man to mourn in silence this unnecessary death and his part in it; but the sight of the coffin brought anger instead. He drew his eyes away. In the dry watercourse, beyond the olives on Bob's land, the dam's empty grey wall cut a gash in the hills. The sky was drained, the earth parched. When he looked again, the coffin was coming out of the shade and starting the long ascent.

The sharecropper's voice came at him again:

'They'll cut that tree down. The señorita has given permission, they say. Poor man, after what she did to him.'

'The water,' the foreigner mumbled. 'He wanted work …'

The old man didn't hear. 'She forced him to go back on the deal, break his word.' He swore. 'Who'd sharecrop for her?'

'There's plenty would,' said the voice of another who had approached unheard. 'Now Miguel's gone, you'll see. El Mayorazgo is her best farm.'

'Be that as it may, she'll break any sharecropper who takes it on.'

They looked down. The coffin swayed on the mule track, the men's shoulders moving together under the weight, their sandals kicking up dust. At each turn of the traverse they struggled to bring the coffin round.

'They say it had nothing to do with the deal,' the second man said suddenly. 'It was because his betrothed broke off their engagement.'

'Ech! What man kills himself for a woman!' the old man replied.

The foreigner started to say something, but the others were arguing and paid no heed. Shoulders straining, the coffin was making its painful way up the last traverse. No words came to his mind, not even a whispered farewell. He turned to go, the incipient fever misting his vision, and staggered a few steps before recovering sufficiently to walk down the whitewashed street to the square. Recognizing the symptoms, he leant against the fountain's stone lip where the water once flowed, and felt reality fall away. Before he knew it, Bob was beside him, leading him by the arm into the bar and putting a brandy in front of him.

'You look as if you need it. What's wrong, John?'

He felt the liquid burning his stomach, knowing it was the worst thing he could take, and managed a smile.

'It's the Suez sickness …'

Bob looked at him, wondering if this was one of those

newspaper jokes. John was the Oxbridge type he normally didn't have time for unless he was a client. A proper illness ought to have a proper name. But there wasn't any doubt he was ill, he'd seen him through the bar window clinging to the fountain as though he was about to fall.

'It's probably the sun. You ought to wear a hat ... Anyway, I've got a bit of good news that'll cheer you up. María Burgos has agreed a deal for the channel across her land. We'll get the water to the dam in a couple of weeks. The worst's over now. You'll see, we'll put this place on the map.'

'Ah!' Behind Bob's head the faded advertisement turned grey, the monkey on the bottle, ANIS DEL MONO, and above, hanging from the beams, the legs of ham like dusty stones. 'Bob, haven't you heard? About Miguel Alarcón?'

'Who? Oh, the man who committed suicide. Yes, I heard, terrible thing.'

'He was the one I told you about. He wanted work on the dam.'

'That's who it was. I remember. Still, he wouldn't have killed himself over that; there are plenty of people who need work here. Ah, there's Salvador.'

The foreman's deeply lined face appeared at the bar. Behind him were the half dozen men working on the dam. Bob said he had been down to the site and found no one there. The foreman's hemp sandals stirred on the tiles.

'Sí, señor Bob, it's the custom for a funeral. Miguel Alarcón was buried this afternoon.'

'Buried?' sniggered one of the workmen.

Bob asked if he knew why he had killed himself.

'They say María Burgos, his landlord, made Miguel break off a deal to sell a calf to a neighbour. Because of the drought he couldn't grow enough fodder to keep it. To break a deal, señor, is to betray your word as a man ...'

'No, it was the girl, I tell you,' broke in the tall workman.

'Qué va, hombre! Miguel wasn't the sort ...'

The voices circled repetitively, fused, going nowhere. More men pushed into the bar. Beyond them, in the square, the simpleton's dark profiled face and white raincoat paced back and forth in front of a crowd of men who suddenly fell back before a black-clothed figure: eyes fixed as always, Bible held close to his chest, his narrow strides carried him past as though the men didn't exist. Instead of turning as usual to pace back again, he vanished into his house, the studded door slamming behind him.

'He knows no shame.'

The men's voices were sullen, anonymous now. 'He made them take the back streets to the cemetery. The mayor wouldn't let the coffin through. They pulled stones out to make a hole in the wall to push through ... Ay! They buried him like a dog ...'

It was then that John's head seemed to empty out and his legs gave way. He knew what was about to happen and clutched at the bar.

2

Dolores gave a little cry and ran forward. With Bob's help she laid him on the iron bedstead; his eyes were closed and his face drained of colour. The coldness of his limbs and his whispered, insistent refusal of a doctor surprised her. What if he died on her hands? His hoarse reassurances did little to calm her: it had happened before, everything would be all right. Looking at him, she wasn't so sure.

For days John lay so motionless that when she peered round the door she feared the worst. His eyes were always shut and, afraid he'd stopped breathing, she slipped quietly over to the bed. Then, sometimes, he opened his eyes, no more than a chink, and, relieved, she went from the room. She was coming to feel a certain warmth for the young man.

In the six months she had worked for him, they'd barely exchanged more than a few words. He thanked her politely when he came down to eat, punctiliously paying her first for the food she had bought from the market in the morning, then opening a book without seeming to notice what he ate. He left everything to her, she could do as she pleased. He spent most of his time in the airless, almost lightless granary hammering away on a typewriter. Always alone. It was enough to make anyone ill. If he recovered, he'd have to live a healthier life, go out, enjoy himself more, like Sr Bob.

His illness made him vulnerable, more human. When she

brought in the broth that was all he would eat, gratitude broke through the formality and reserve of the past. A fleeting smile accompanied his near-voiceless thanks. Once, as she stood by the bed, he attempted to say something. The words came out so muddled that she was confused. 'The men' – what men? – 'couldn't' – 'the dam'. At the end she caught the name Miguel. There was no strength in his voice, his eyes were dull, and perhaps he knew he was making no sense for he collapsed on the pillow motionless again. She straightened the sheet, the room was cool – as cool as she could make it in the sweltering heat – the shutters closed over the glassless windows, and the pitcher of fresh water on the commode. She couldn't do more. Thank God, the heat must soon lessen, the terrible shameless summer end.

Gratefully, John heard the door shut and immediately wished she had remained. At first her constant attention deepened the despair that always accompanied the illness. Depression consumed all sense of being. Engulfed by a permanent stark now, tomorrow – the self of tomorrow, the becoming – collapsed into itself. Life – not the philosophical proposition but his own life – was without meaning. Drifting without compass, horizon or stars, he knew this more intimately than anything.

His only defence was the inertness of driftwood; it prevented him from being plunged to the bottom for good. But nothing could stop the waves of memory washing over him: Miguel by the door, beret in hand, saying the crops had dried up, the calf was going to be sold, asking for a day-labourer's job on the dam.

'You've come to the wrong person,' he heard himself say again. 'The dam's got nothing to do with me.'

'Ah! I thought ...' Miguel's eyes showed both disbelief and acceptance.

'No ... Look, it's only a question of time ... María Burgos can't go on refusing water to her own farms. She's bound to strike a deal.'

John had tried to believe his own words, to inspire Miguel with a confidence he no longer felt. Ever since the village water had dried up three months before, in June, the land had been scalped to the bone by the heat and drought. Bob had rapidly begun work on a borehole that landowners had previously abandoned before striking water, and again it had taken longer than he had expected. He needed water to fill the 25-million-gallon dam he was building. When, in the first week of August, water was at last struck, María Burgos, Miguel's landlord, had demanded a punitive sum from Bob for the right to channel across her land to the dam. In doing so, she had denied water to Miguel and her other sharecroppers. For over three weeks, as intermediaries negotiated about the channel, the newly tapped water had gushed uselessly down a ravine. It was in this situation that Miguel suddenly appeared in John's house to ask for a job on the dam.

'Wait a bit longer. After all these months what's another week or two?'

Miguel stood there in silence, apparently not hearing John's words. And then, down the mountain, came a rush of hot wind and the foolscap pages on the table went flying. John had scampered to pick them up, relieved not to have to say more. Miguel was confused, bending to gather up sheets round his feet. John wanted him to go. 'All right,' he'd said at last, 'I know Bob isn't taking anyone on at the moment. The way things are with María Burgos there's no point. But I'll ask him for you. Tomorrow …'

Miguel's hand was on the door. Through the roar of the wind, John heard his footsteps on the stairs and began ordering the typewritten sheets. The next day, true enough, he had mentioned it to Bob, but without pressing the matter. He could, should have said, take him on, he needs it, pay him out of what you owe me. It's only five bob a day.

But he hadn't. The idea hadn't even occurred to him. And a few days later Miguel was dead.

3

John struggled to raise himself on the straw pillow. The depression brought rage in its wake: rage at Miguel for implicating him in his death, for taking his revenge in so accusing and uncontestable a way. Christ, a few days was all he had to wait! Last Monday, the day he killed himself, María Burgos and Bob reached agreement. He had died without knowing it. Why couldn't he wait?

The rage was so intense that, in a small lucid space beneath, he saw its irrationality. He was raging at Miguel to deny his own inevitable sense of guilt. A job on the dam would have given him breathing space, saved his life. That was all he'd asked of a friend. The final straw in a summer of disasters. And he'd been turned away.

John cried, overcome with remorse. The tears, for once, silenced the other self that normally watched him. He slumped in the bed, not caring whether Dolores discovered him in this state.

He must have cried himself to sleep because suddenly he awoke sweating with the thought already formed: it was *she*, wasn't it, who'd cut off hope. María Burgos! Refusing him water, breaking the deal when she'd left him no option but to sell the calf, she had shown nothing but disdain for his plight. Yes, it was she who had to carry the blame for his suicide.

John lay back in relief. Pushing a fringe of matted hair from his eyes, a small fissure opened in the back wall of his mind. If it hadn't been for the dam, would she have acted like that? In those long waterless months, wasn't that the real cause of this nightmare: the dam? Bob's grandiose plans? Hadn't Miguel always predicted her almost certain reaction against it – and most probably at his cost?

But what was it then the other men had said? A quarrel with his betrothed. What betrothed? Miguel had never spoken about being engaged.

John attempted to control the thoughts that chased, mouth to tail, behind his closed eyelids. To give them an order, a causality that would, once and for all, assign them their proper responsibility. Even as he tried, they turned on him: the ordering of things seemed no more than another way of denying guilt.

'Dolores!' he called, but his voice was too weak.

He wiped the sweat from his eyes. He needed her to slow down the thoughts, her presence soothed him. With a patience he, of all people, had no right to expect, Dolores looked after him as no one else had. She never asked what was wrong, what illness he had. He'd been shunted through enough London hospital departments to know that no doctor could tell him. An illness without a medical name was an illness that didn't exist. Everyone needed a medical name to feel safe. Everyone, except Dolores.

He heard her breaking brushwood in the kitchen and called out again; but the cracking and swishing of rosemary went on as before.

Once more he tried to order his thoughts and, as though its underpinnings were giving way, his head threatened to collapse. He recognized the symptom: it was how the illness had started. He'd staggered back to the office after an attack of flu to find that his closest friend, Dave, had resigned over the paper's policy on the Suez crisis. He had wanted to follow him. The editor's chauvinist fervour sickened him, but he'd been sickened still more by his own lack of resolve in writing the leaders demanded. ('This newspaper, this country will not stand by while another petty dictator tears up international agreements ...') Yet his only act of defiance had been to bet the editor ten shillings that Eden would be out of power within a couple of months. He had never collected his money because on the day of his return to the office he had had his first collapse.

He reached out for the water jug but it was too heavy to lift. The total exhaustion was like an unending flu. Each time he'd recovered and gone back to work, his head had drained away on the editorial floor. At last, with a paternal pat on the back, the editor had told him to take an extended holiday; his job would be waiting for him on his return. He hadn't called it sick leave, John had noted, too worn out to smile but grateful to be leaving, he didn't know where. Somewhere, anywhere, so long as he could find a time in which not to have to think on command.

Nothing here, he thought, trying to read patterns in the cracked blue wash above the bed, had come between him and himself. In the six months that he'd spent in Benalamar the sickness had vanished. Every morning, in the muddy light of the granary, he'd sat at his typewriter, convinced of the need to discover in his ordinary enough English middle-class childhood the fatal flaw that would explain his passivity. To find it was the task he'd set himself from the day of his arrival in the village last March; and until he had done so he intended to stay in Benalamar. The flaw's most recent manifestation could be summed up in a few words: where Dave acted, he, John, fell ill ... But this syndrome, which had served as the starting point of his self-examination, had not as yet led to the vital discovery – or in consequence to the cure. For the question was not just to discover the flaw but to expel it, like a foreign object, from his being.

With a conviction bordering on the fanatic, he believed that writing was the only possible means of achieving both aims. Once the flaw had been pinned down in words, exactly defined, it would be a relatively easy task to uproot it in himself. This fiction, fed by his youthful knowledge of books rather than life, had at least once a fortnight led him to think that he had definitively impaled the flaw on a shaft of words. Leaning back in his chair, he would examine it with satisfied curiosity until, to his horror, he saw it diffusing like a blot of ink across the page, lacking precision, contour, content, the amplitude to take in all exceptions. He hadn't been discouraged. The following morning found him again at the granary table. Was it not Flaubert who had said that inspiration consisted of taking one's place at one's desk every day at the same hour?

On the ochre wall above the table he had pinned a cutting from *The Times*: 'It was when I faced the British invasion that I felt what that icy, effortless indifference and superiority in Englishmen like myself had done to the rest of the world ...' They were words he wished he had written himself. Each time he had read them he'd hunched over the typewriter with renewed passion until, with the daily ration of pages achieved, he allowed himself to plan his afternoon walk, preferring the solitariness of the countryside to the village, a solitariness almost unbroken until he encountered Miguel.

On those spring afternoons down at El Mayorazgo, watching the water flow like liquid mercury through the channels and furrows Miguel geometrically hoed, the earth turning black round the tomato vines, he had been filled with a child-like stillness he thought he had forgotten. The air was heat-stilled, the hills shimmered under an implacable sun, a mineral silence fell on the earth. Up above the three pines on the hill, the ascending white lines of the village were drained of colour. Riveted by the heat and the water's flow or the arc of Miguel's hoe through the air, John watched him from the shade of a carob. As still and enduring as the land's hot silence, it seemed, Miguel's face under the sombrero looked up with the same quiet words, the same slight smile ...

He shut his eyes. Again he had been a passive observer, refusing to commit himself. Even to an elementary act of human kindness when Miguel needed it most. That was the truth, that's why it had come to this. He felt himself going under.

'Dolores!'

'Sí, señor.' She stood in the doorway at last.

'Please, could you fetch me a glass of water. And open the shutters.'

The light hurt John's eyes, but it was better than the perpetual penumbra. The water was cool and he drank it gratefully. Dolores watched him, thinking he was looking better, his blue eyes less dull. Feeling the warmth of her gaze, John looked at her: dark hair, fine features – but how lined her face was, how old could she be? Not more than forty, surely. He gave her the glass. 'Thank you, Dolores. Thank you for everything.' She smiled, stood as though waiting, and he searched for something more to say; in the end all he could find was to ask whether the farms were getting water now,

'No. Miguel's mother is bringing charges against the building of the dam.'

'Charges! What charges? Against whom?'

'I don't know. She says the dam is unsafe, that it's responsible for Miguel's death. You heard how they buried him? Ay! They wouldn't have dared if he had been rich. But the rich don't kill themselves, those who have money can do what they want.' Her voice was harsh, monotonous like the land burnt by the sun.

'It doesn't matter to him now.'

'He was a man, señor, even in death the poor have a right ...' From outside came the familiar cries of the fish-vendor, the waterman with his donkey, the blind lottery-seller. Dolores's voice fell to a whisper. 'They killed him, señor, and buried him like an animal.'

'They, Dolores? Who do you mean?'

'They … No, the señorita, María Burgos. For years she has cheated that family. Didn't she make him go back on the deal after Miguel had given his word? He had to ask Tío Bigote for the calf back. She's without shame.'

'But the water, the dam?' John's voice was so low she barely heard.

'If she had wanted he could have had water. Hasn't the water been flowing since San Jenaro's day? María Burgos used the dam to get money out of Sr Bob. She didn't care about Miguel or anyone else.'

'If it hadn't been for the dam, he'd have had water, is that what you're saying, Dolores?'

'I don't know. Perhaps she'd have found something else. But that's what Miguel's mother thinks.'

'And so she's bringing charges.' She nodded. There was a long silence. Finally John summoned the courage to add: 'Perhaps there were other reasons.'

'You mean Juana, his betrothed?'

'Well, yes …' She didn't understand, didn't know that Miguel had asked him for a job. Sinking back on the pillow, closing his eyes, John barely heard her reply.

4

At dawn, as the donkeys' hooves clipped over the cobbles under his window, John awoke to an unexpected surge of energy. He lay still for a while. In the past this sudden flow had sometimes been a false augury and drained away as rapidly as it had come. But now, under its sustaining power, he got up and went into the granary next door. Shining through the small window, the first rays of the sun lit the adobe ceiling and the beams of dried agave shoots and fell in a blood-red patch on the tiled floor.

He stared uncomprehendingly at the sheet of paper in the typewriter; the words it contained seemed meaningless. How was it that, in apparently so short a time, they had drained of all content? Was it the sickness, he wondered, realizing that he had no exact idea of how long he had been ill. He looked for a calendar. *Saturday, 9 September*, it must be, at a guess, because yesterday was almost certainly a Friday – Dolores had said there was only fish to be had. Twelve days of illness, twelve days then since Miguel died and was buried: Monday, 28 August, he'd never forget. Twelve days, no time at all, and yet it felt like eternity.

He leafed through the typewritten sheets stacked on the table and then put them on the floor. The self-examination that had engaged so much of his energy seemed suddenly irrelevant. For a long while he sat staring at the clean sheet he had put in the machine; he knew he had to write about Miguel, to uncover cause and effect in order finally to be able to accept his death. Who could have believed six months ago that this calm, smiling man would kill himself? John stared at the paper: where to begin?

The things before they were known, he typed at last, *the things once known … The problem is always the same – to reason, to become aware …*

Underneath, he added: Cesare Pavese, his diary.

Then: How can one understand the things before they are known? Seen from outside, everything is relative, equal – equally absurd or gratuitous – without a meaning other than what one wants to give it. Beautiful even. I remember, for example (things before they were known), when one afternoon in the shade of a tree, I was roused from half-sleep and sat up to look, to take pleasure in watching something unknown, becoming aware slowly of movement and sound, a whirring of stones that fell with a thud in the corn. Rippling, the thin stalks closed over the sound. The afternoon sun lay full on the terrace, leaving only a patch of shade under an olive where the man stood; beyond, like liquefied heat, the vapour shimmered over the hills. The man bent again, fastening the stone, and his arm looped in a slow circle which gathered speed until the stone was released with the crack of a rifle. Then he stood motionless, watching. In the corn nothing happened, a few birds fluttered, there was silence again. I lay back against the tree. Every few minutes the man stooped for a stone to send through the sunlight; an hour passed. The stones fell in a wide arc, as though pursuing a pattern, varied indefinitely, aimed by the slow, deliberate movement under the tree. Then a girl appeared round the back of the farmstead, across the terrace from him, and started to clap. The rhythm was fast and insistent and the sound reverberated in the hills. The stones continued to whirl and crash more rapidly than before, as though the girl's quick beat had sharpened the urgency, but neither showed any awareness of the other's presence. In the corn nothing moved. The girl faced the terrace, her clapping directed at it with ferocious monotony, her hands at the height of her face. A woman in black came out of the house and took her place next to the girl and started to beat on a tin can. She held a stick in one hand. The stones flailed into the dry earth under the stalks. Now the man started to shout, long hoarse cries that rang out over the beating of the old woman's tin, over the girl's shrill cries, up to the pines. The three stood facing the corn, concentrated on something under the vast sky, in feverish isolation from the rest of the land, which shimmered in heat-stricken silence. In a movement of incantation, the girl raised her arms above her head and ran forward a few steps as though about to throw herself in the corn. Then she stepped back and began clapping again. She repeated the movements at regular intervals and, as the old woman's drumbeat reached a fury, lunged with outstretched arms and yellow sombrero into the corn. Her red skirt made a splash of ceremonial colour, the shouts and the beating galvanized her dance. Like fragments of silence, a few specks winged away in the sun.

Yet when the thing was explained, the purpose made clear, I saw it unquestioningly, gratefully even, given a distaste for the absurd; the explanation was simple enough.

A stocky man in faded blue trousers, his head on one side, he stood in front of me under the pines. I noticed the sling but didn't recognize him; it must have been several weeks later because I don't remember returning that way until Bob started clearing the watercourse in preparation for the dam. There was water still, splashing over a drystone wall and onto the track where it ran to waste. More dripped through the joints in the strips of guttering that carried the flow over the watercourse where the white sand absorbed it. On the low hill, the earth was crumbling shale or perhaps it was earth becoming rock again; the umbrella pines made a fragrant shade. I sat looking at the small farmstead in the hollow below, at the terrace of corn where nothing moved.

His 'buenas tardes' startled me from a half sleep in which I had become part of the hot afternoon silence. He seemed to be smiling, but then it didn't seem so. 'Resting? It's cool under these pines.' He sat on his haunches looking at me. His eyes were cool, they took in my lightweight trousers and drip-dry shirt, and I got up.

'Excuse me, is this your land?'

'Mine or anyone else's, it makes no difference. You're from the village?'

I nodded. Under the sombrero his face was dark, high-cheekboned. His eyes were blue. 'I saw you, I remember now, using that thing one afternoon in the corn. I couldn't make out what you were doing.'

'Ah!' He held out the sling as though I were questioning it. 'Sparrows.' He must have seen my face because he repeated it.

I laughed. 'You mean ...'

'Look!' Out of the sun, in a swoop of black specks, a flock of birds dropped on the corn, the stalks quivering as they picked the ears. He bent for a stone and the sling whirled, exploding with a crack. 'At this rate there won't be an ear left.' Then after a time he added: 'The crop isn't worth anything, there hasn't been any rain.'

'And that's the only way to keep the birds off?'

He glanced at me questioningly, I remember. 'Yes.' Then he laughed a rolling laugh I came to know, as though the idea had just struck him. 'They don't leave you in peace.'

The sun slanted across his face under the hat as we stood looking down at the farmstead, a low, whitewashed cottage with pitched roofs of moss green and red rounded tiles. Below it the terraces, not more than a few feet across, fell away to the bowl where the earth was cross-hatched with a pattern of furrows. I let my eyes linger on the design: a central ridge, darkened by shadow, from which the furrows branched out in parallel curves to another dark line from which their curve was reversed. From here on the hill it was like a geometric composition in earth. The soil looked good.

Average, he said, as long as there was water. He turned towards the mountains as though a cloud might appear. Their colour had changed from vermilion to purple and the sun caught the haze that lay in their folds, silhouetting range upon range against an empty sky. He shrugged his shoulders. They were stooped too, but broader than mine; beside him I always felt gangly. In his heavy hemp sandals the colour of earth, he stood there as though he had grown out of the land.

Below, a figure in black came out of the house and looked through the olives and almonds along the edge of the terrace. When she shouted, it was a harsh, drawn-out cry. Mi-gu-el! His voice answered hers, turning the 'voy' into a full-throated cry that carried to the hills. He laughed. 'Well, it's time, adió!' and he picked up the digging hoe he had leant against the tree and moved down the hillside, very light on his feet, as though the rocks and stones were footholds in the earth.

5

There was a knock at the granary door and Dolores's face appeared. 'But señor, what are you doing? And in here too, where it is already so hot!' Her words, her face suggested that she had seen the Resurrection, and as though to confirm it, John got out of his chair.

'I'm feeling better, thank you,' he said, but she would have none of it, and insisted on bustling him into the front room where it was cooler.

'You must be more careful, you've been very ill. And now I'll make you your breakfast.'

As she went into the kitchen she thought, once again, how much he looked like the few Englishmen she'd seen in the picture magazines that occasionally reached the village from Madrid. The blond hair swept back from his forehead, his broad-set blue eyes and straight nose … But the lower half of his face seemed to have come from another mould: his mouth and chin were weakly filled in, as though the mould hadn't had time to set.

Her observation would not have surprised John, who had often remarked, as though his inner flaw were a visible stigma, on the fleeting aspect of his jaw and chin, and had thought of growing a beard to hide it. But inertia, abetted perhaps by the fact that beards were unfashionable, had kept him from disguising himself.

Idly waiting for her to return, he picked up the book closest to hand and turned the pages. It was one of the many he had read lying in the shade of a eucalyptus or pine – Sartre's *Baudelaire* – on his afternoon walks, and his eye now caught a sentence he had underlined: *If, contrary to received opinion, men only ever had the life they deserved* ... Again the phrase brought on vertigo: could it be true? Everything that happened was a choice of the self, an ineluctable destiny spun out of scores, thousands of decisions, small and large? A life made behind one's back, as it were. Was it true – true of Miguel?

Agitatedly John paced up and down the small room. No – such a view took no account of what had been done to him; on the other hand, it was he, Miguel, who had chosen ... Chosen? Did one choose ...?

Dolores's return broke into his chaotic thoughts. Drinking the barley coffee and goat's milk, spreading the waxy, yellow margarine on the bread, he tried to push these thoughts down: what was the use, one would never know now. Dolores was still hovering, as though afraid to leave him alone.

'Dolores, did Ana come here one day?' he asked suddenly.

'Ana?'

'Yes, Ana, Miguel's sister. Before all this happened.'

'Ah, she passed by one day, I remember, yes. She stopped to talk. She was going to the shop for material for a new dress she was going to make for the *feria*. Poor thing, she won't be able to wear it now.'

'Oh! She didn't say anything about wanting to see me?'

'No.' Dolores bent to take the coffee glass from the table, looking puzzled; but she didn't ask, why this question? Any more than Miguel had ever questioned a question. At that moment a motorbike's roar obliterated the morning calm, followed shortly by a determined rap on the door, and Bob walked in without waiting for an answer.

'Well, John, how're you feeling? Better by the looks of it. That's good. I meant to come by yesterday only I was laying out the channel.' He accepted the coffee Dolores offered him, sat down on the creaky wood-and-rush chair and looked at John. 'The dam will be finished in a month. I put another six men on yesterday.'

'More men!'

'Yes, they're working piece rates, it'll come out quicker and cheaper this way.'

'But Bob!'

'But what?'

'I was thinking about Miguel Alarcón. Christ, that's all he wanted and you said there wasn't a job.'

'Oh yes. Well, we hadn't got María Burgos's agreement then, had we?' His eyes met John's. 'I heard more about it yesterday, John. It was definitely because the girl jilted him, there's no doubt at all, everyone says so. He had been acting strangely since she threw him over.'

'His mother's bringing charges, did you know?'

'So rumour has it. You know how people here talk. In fact I hope it's true. That funeral was scandalous, like something out of the Middle Ages. It's bad enough throwing the bones out of the cemetery when the relatives can't pay.' His eyes narrowed, as they did when he contemplated an injustice, then as suddenly flashed in his broad, sunburnt face. 'I'd like to see the priest and the mayor sacked, the bastards.'

'Little hope of that, I should think,' John answered tartly. 'Franco's Spain isn't exactly a democracy, is it?' For some reason he regretted his sharpness of tone. Evidently Bob didn't know what Dolores had told him. I shan't tell him either, John thought. 'And the water? You really think that had nothing to do with Miguel's suicide?'

'No. They're used to that sort of thing, they've always had droughts.'

He shook his head. 'I'm not so sure, Bob, I want to find out.'

'Ask the people, they'll tell you. And even supposing it was the water, you know it can't happen again, not with the dam.'

'That doesn't help him.'

'Oh, for fuck's sake, John, you're becoming obsessed just because you happened to know him.' His tone was cutting, contemptuous.

'Maybe. But this wasn't part of the plan, was it?'

Another sharp answer was forming on Bob's tongue when he thought better of it. 'You've been ill, John, that's the trouble. You'll see things differently when you're better. Listen, I think I'll be able to get some of the men started on my house in a couple of weeks. I had an idea the other day for yours, it'll fit nicely on the site. I'll show you when you come down.'

Before John could think what to say, Bob was gone, hammering down the stairs; and soon the roar of his motorbike was sending sound waves reverberating down the narrow street.

II. Water

6

Perhaps Bob is right, perhaps it's becoming an obsession. If I hadn't known Miguel, if he hadn't come up to ask for help, this past would remain a perpetual, indifferent present. But now the present has reordered the past, given it new meanings. Like Suez. That's what Pavese's phrase really means. My life has come out of books; the written seems more real than what I live. Bob isn't like that, I suppose it's what I admire in him. But now he feels I am obsessively betraying the past, one he thought I shared with him. I can't help it, I have to know.

Had I been more aware, I see now, there were things I could have understood then, but they seemed to make so little difference: a pitcher of water a day which Dolores fetched, which was in its place under the washstand, I didn't need more. Water, I remember, to be taken for granted, like the hills and the heat, like the hole in the square we peered down one morning in early June, the men who had gathered at the news making way for the two foreigners to look, as though eyes could tap the source in the mountain and restore the flow. So this was where the water had come from, this hole under the slab I had so often crossed on my way down to see Miguel, and now, as mysteriously, no longer appeared. We crowded round uselessly to look at the echoing tunnel whose rough-hewn dry walls were already warm, the men's faces worn as though the earth had got under the skin. And then someone said:

'They'll deepen the borehole.'

And another: 'What's the use, this one has always given out.'

And a third: 'It's the señorita's new borehole that's taken the water.'

'Hombre! She hasn't hit water either.'

All round us their voices came in short, heavy bursts; they didn't move when they spoke. The sun was full on the square, on their threadbare cotton trousers and shirts, their earth-coloured sombreros. As though simulating a passion to break the dead hours of waiting for work, they repeated the same arguments again and again. There was nothing to be done. Water, or the lack of it, were facts of nature, immutable.

Idly my mind turned to Miguel. He had been right, the water hadn't lasted, I wasn't going to see the terraces flowing with water again.

Bob took my arm, leading me clear.

'Well, that's that, isn't it?' I said. 'That's the end of the dam.'

'No. Look, there's the other borehole, the one that bloke – what's his name? Miguel, that's right – told you about. I've been out there to look at it. They didn't hit water as quickly as they expected, and they've run out of money. A lot of the owners, including María Burgos, wouldn't put any more money in, so the drilling has stopped. I'm going to see about it.' In a few quick strides he was across the square, calling over his shoulder, 'Stop by tonight,' and for a moment, watching his broad-shouldered figure disappear, I was moved by his unquenchable spirit. Ah well, he had his reasons, I thought, his land, a house to build ...

I turned to go, an unfinished page waiting for me in the granary. Crossing the beaten-earth square, I recalled my arrival three months earlier by taxi, a 1929 Buick that bounced and groaned its way up from the coast and finally steamed to a triumphant halt by these bitter orange trees. In Torre del Mar, on the coast, a few English were living; I'd no desire to be another exile among them and was leaving after a few days. It was early March but the sun already seemed to have the weight of summer.

Cursing the potholes and a foreigner's whim, the driver's sole exclamation of pleasure, more to himself than to me, came at the sight of water foaming down the side of the dirt road, where figures in black, bent over their washing, stood up and stared, following the car's slow ascent, and children and dogs rushed out of a farmhouse. I followed the water, like quicksilver in the sun, seeing the two Guardia Civil in their black tricornes and uniforms the colour of the agave they stood beside, turning their heads slowly in the cloud of dust to watch as the taxi took a curve. And there, opening below, was a bowl of earth, cross-hatched with furrows, where a man stood staring up at the road. Behind was a white farmstead, like all the rest, and a hill with three umbrella pines. It might have been Miguel, though I can't be sure, I was looking more at the earth than at the man. A half dozen more curves and suddenly, like a vision of Braque, the village appeared – a series of dazzling white cubes and sienna-brown tiles piled at random angles up the sides of a hill that rose steeply to a ruined fortress or church at the top. I gasped. Beyond, range upon range of mountains etched in vermilion and shadowed blues against the afternoon sky.

The taxi plunged into a narrow cobbled street, there was a flow of white and sunlight ricocheting off walls, the sudden glimpse of jasmine in a darkened patio, a figure in black caught in the sun, and then the curving down to the square where pools of shadow lay under the orange trees.

Dazzled by whiteness and a sense of enclosure as people gathered round to stare, I was disconcerted to see an English face push through the crowd. 'They don't see many cars up here,' an unmistakably North London voice said. 'And even fewer foreigners.'

He picked up my typewriter and led me into the bar. His square-cut features, the chin especially, and the broad nose made me think of a boxer; his eyes were a very pale blue, slightly sharp. He was evidently at home in the bar, and two beers and tapas of some undeterminable meat appeared instantly. He asked where I was from, and said he came from Camden Town, a surveyor turned estate agent who'd done well, so I was led to understand, out of the recent property boom. Camden Town was coming up. 'But I've had enough. A bit of the quiet life is what I need now. I've bought some land here, got it pretty cheap, and I'm going to build myself a house.'

And I, thinking the light in the bar was like weathered wood, taking in the faded Manolete poster, the Mono advertisement, the dusty hams hanging from the beams, only half listened. Everything seemed covered in an air of fragrant desuetude and freshness at once. For the first time since leaving London I knew I had chosen right. I looked through the door to where two or three men sat in pyjama tops and others stood in the shade of the wall, saw the white walls broken by barred rectangles and squares, felt the world dropping away in the afternoon sun.

My thoughts were interrupted by his asking if I had somewhere to stay. No, I confessed, taken aback by my lack of prevision. Well, he could fix it. He called the bar owner and began a rapid-fire negotiation. 'Can you make ten bob a day? Yes. OK. You'll like this house, needs a bit of doing up, bit primitive, but you won't get much better here. Come on …'

And so, thanks to Bob, I found myself in possession of two furnished rooms, the granary, a waterless, seatless lavatory in a bare room large enough to swing several cats, and a kitchen. It was the granary that won my heart, and I quickly moved in a table and chair and set up my typewriter. My happiness at being so rapidly installed was mixed with a measure of irritation at being immediately indebted to Bob.

The next morning Dolores appeared; again, Bob seemed to have made the arrangements, if I understood her correctly. I determined in future to keep to myself; with the start of the promised self-examination, I had plenty to occupy me.

A week or so after my arrival, he dropped in. 'Haven't seen you around. What've you been doing with yourself?' I mumbled some excuse. 'Well, come up for a meal tonight. You know where my place is? Last but one house.'

I had no ready excuse and that evening I found myself sitting on the terrace of the old house he had rented, more spacious, though not better equipped, than mine. I thanked him for finding me Dolores. Bob laughed.

'Does she come on her own? Yes? Perhaps they're getting used to us.'

He'd been hard pushed at the beginning to find anyone, he recalled: it was almost impossible to get a village woman to work for a man on his own. Until his wife came out, his cook always came chaperoned by a young girl. So he'd taken the trouble of asking his cook, who had persuaded her cousin Dolores to take on the job. 'Now that June's gone back to London for a visit I half expect to see the chaperone turn up again.'

He refilled my glass and began to describe the house he was planning to build. Water was one of the main problems. At the moment there was plenty and it ran to waste in the watercourse because no one was irrigating – it was, as I've said, not yet quite spring. But for three or four months in the summer there was never enough. It was scandalous. 'I can't understand why they don't do something about it. Eight months of waste and four months of shortage. And this has been the third dry winter in a row.'

At that moment the men carrying bales of brushwood on their heads started to come by. Narrowing, Bob's eyes watched this strange and pitiful procession bent so low under the weight that only the men's feet dragging in the dust showed. We had both seen it before and yet it never failed to leave its mark. I knew such poverty existed, had even written about aid to the Third World, but I'd never seen it until coming here, that was the difference.

'You know how far they carry that wood?' Bob asked, breaking the silence. From the top of the mountains, three hours' walk. And as if that wasn't enough, they had to hawk the firewood from door to door when they got to the village, often forced to exchange it for a bit of bread. For a while, until the last man had gone, there was silence again.

'We were poor, I remember that as a kid before the war,' he said suddenly. 'My father was out of work a lot of the time. Still was when I went into the RAF in 1940. We didn't have that much to eat, but it was never like this.'

For a moment I hoped he would leave it at that, but he went on, talking of the men who stand uselessly in the square waiting for work that never comes; of the carriers running fish up from the coast in sacks strapped round their foreheads; of men who are beaten up in the Guardia Civil barracks for gathering wild esparto grass in the mountains to keep themselves alive – esparto that a well-known falangist in the town claims as his private property ...

He glanced at me; I saw now that the day when, on an impulse, I disembarked in Gibraltar from the Alexandria-bound freighter, I hadn't given a thought to the present. I felt better and I'd had enough of the sea, the cramped quarters, needed to feel land under my feet again. And it was the past of the civil war that had once interested me ...

'Living here brings you up short. Did you hear what

{38}

Macmillan said the other day? We've never had it so good in Britain, he said. No thanks to him and his Tories, it was Labour, the Welfare State we can thank for that. It's something I'll never forget, the first time I voted. They could do with a bit of that here.'

In the last evening light the land fell away in front of us: scattered terraces of barley and alfalfa shone green among the soft, barren hills, and isolated trees were in flower along their edges. If all the land were as fertile as those terraces, Bob said. And why not? The water so arduously mined from the mountain, in the way learnt from the Moors, was wasted, not conserved … With enough water there'd be enough work – and suddenly surging forward into the idea of a reservoir, Bob carried me on into valleys green with alfalfa, covered by fruit trees, rich with cattle, where there would be work for all. An end to drought. His eyes shone with the vision; this dry, cracking earth made green, farmers exporting their crops; and he – no, now it was us – in this swollen dream surveying the meaning of our presence here. A revolution of water and work; the desert blooming in a joyful Swiss scene that was darkened by an uncomfortable thought: hadn't he just shown me a model of his house, hadn't it a waterflow through it? A gallery with a fountain, a pool?

He smiled. 'That's right. What gets done in this world without a bit of self-interest? It's human nature after all.' But he wouldn't need a tenth of the reservoir, the rest would go to the farms. 'Twenty-five million gallons. The watercourse goes through my land, and I'm going to build a dam. It'll put an end to this stupid situation, help the people to help themselves. It's a good investment all round, good for the village, good for everyone.'

Struck by the logic of it, infused by the dream, I couldn't help then but agree. Yet simultaneously a nub of doubt formed; Bob's frankness about his motives was perhaps a little too frank for my taste, but this was of less concern than the fear of allowing myself to get carried away by schemes that would distract from my self-examination. For all my expressions of agreement, I knew that I wouldn't fully involve myself in his plans. I wasn't capable of sustaining his sort of vision. As usual, I'd be an observer.

7

11 September

Bob was in a hurry, and had men scraping and blasting rock in the watercourse. His hope was to build fast enough to catch some of the water running to waste before the irrigating season fully began. There was little time, just enough to build a single retaining wall to hold a few million gallons; the second, exterior wall would have to come later. He couldn't know then that, within two months, there'd be no water at all. But Miguel knew that the flow was lessening.

Once the work in the watercourse began, I used to go down through the hills most afternoons and past the dam site to El Mayorazgo half a mile below. Aware from a distance of my approach, Miguel made no sign that he'd seen me, and my advance became tentative to the point of turning back. He continued to look absorbed in the maize or tomatoes at his feet. When I was only a few feet away, he'd turn, saying, 'Hola! Out for a walk?' or something like that. A slight, diffident smile sometimes. 'It's hot for walking today,' he'd add, seeming to understand the need but not the choice of the hottest part of the day. And I'd reply, the heat was what I liked, it was why I'd come here, which was not the whole truth or even a part, but what could I tell him?

Perhaps it was because I was brought up in a countryside where greens fade into greens and villages melt into valleys that I liked the bold contours of this parched land, the small, precise terraces cut out of the hills on top of which, dominating the countryside, the villages stand. I'd left that other countryside as soon as I could. It said nothing to me; nor, to my father's despair, did his solicitor's practice in the neighbouring town. But in this landscape I felt at home, it freed something in me, though I was never able to explain it to Miguel.

I'd sit at the edge of the terrace watching him hoe the green stalks of maize or tie up tomatoes; occasionally I'd ask about the crops he was growing and he, I remember, often laughed, looking at me curiously, his head to one side, as though such questions had never been asked. Breaking off an unwanted stem or changing the water's flow with a quick scoop of his hoe, he'd say, 'Well, it's not the custom' or something of the kind.

He demanded nothing of me nor I of him. What, it seemed then, would he have demanded of me, he who was so apparently self-contained, who was always working? Even his stillness seemed activity somehow.

He was irrigating already, I remember, an early crop of tomatoes and maize. It was this I most liked to watch. He talked more, had little to do but watch the water splash onto the terrace and flow steadily between the diagonal furrows. The water worked for him, maybe that's why. One afternoon, I remember, we went together, he with his hoe over his shoulder, walking slowly, deliberately up the hill and through the pines until we came to the boulder where, only a couple of weeks ago, the men carrying his coffin stopped to change shoulders. Resting there, we looked across at Bob's land and I remember him saying that it was a shame to leave it untilled. It was good land, had grown good crops in the past, and this year not even the olives had been picked. I agreed; I couldn't understand

Bob's neglect. Yet in front of Miguel I became oddly defensive, as though implicated in Bob's indifference, and said something evasive to which he didn't reply.

Swinging his hoe into the damp earth by the boulder, he scooped out the mud to divert the water which backed up bubbling, beginning its flow in the earth channel. He took out a handkerchief and wiped his forehead, pushing the sombrero back over his black hair, and I felt the sweat running uselessly down the back of my neck. 'It's hot today,' he said, and we started back. The water nudged its way along the ditch, barely a foot wide, filling the heat cracks, soaking into the dry bottom in a sluggish flow preceded by small heaps of debris that were overtaken by the faster rush, the water turning clearer, till stopped by a stone which Miguel hooked out, his hoe working to scrape and patch. Haphazardly following the terrain, the ditch disappeared into an expanse of white stones and the water slowed, gurgled and vanished.

'There's half an hour's water lost before it reaches El Mayorazgo.' We paused, Miguel's hoe scraped at the stone, then he walked on. Most of the water drained away there, he said over his shoulder, and I asked why they didn't put in pipes or something, and he replied that there had been talk of it but the landowners couldn't agree. The earth crumbled under our feet, we slid down it to the terraces and sat in the shade waiting for the water to come down the chute in the rock and tentatively ripple out in the earth. My eyes followed the pattern which wound back and forth, losing themselves in the dark lines where the water flowed and which bore to the dry ridges an exact relationship I wanted to grasp until I was aware only of the furrows fusing with my gaze.

The shout rang out from somewhere below and I struggled up. Miguel was standing in the middle of the terrace, the hoe over his shoulder. There was still a narrow plot beside the house that was dry; by now the flow was running round the edge of the terrace, dammed with a scoop of mud, and disappearing over the stone wall to the farmstead below. Coming over to me he remarked, casually it seemed, 'The water won't hold out the summer.' His head was held to one side, eyes motionless under raised eyebrows – an expression that sometimes seemed like an exclamation mark printed on his face, but at other times more like an unspoken question. He hung like that for a moment until, as though waking: 'unless the new borehole ...'

'Oh,' I replied uncertainly, unsure where the water came from.

'It's behind that carob up there,' pointing up to a distant tree on the mountainside; work had been stopped on it some time ago, I heard him say; and then, speaking fast, he added something I didn't understand, which became clear only later, about some people not wanting to lay out money to continue the drilling, though the water was certain. 'It takes a lot of money to dig a borehole,' he concluded.

We moved from the shade and the sun bore down on us with a leaden weight, and perhaps I said 'Oh' or else looked at my watch, thinking of the long, shadeless climb up the track. From the pines, looking back, I saw him below, and heard the sound, like an axe on wood, of his hoe splitting the earth.

8

(When I went down to lunch an hour ago, Dolores, with a certain sternness in her voice, said I ought to go out more. 'The granary is too hot, you'll make yourself ill again.' I reassured her, though I'm not that sure: a dull headache has come back.

She said no more until, bringing in the last plate, she told me people had seen Miguel's mother going into the magistrate's house in Torre del Mar. 'And she didn't have her basket of eggs with her.'

'For God's sake, Dolores, what does that mean?'

'It means she was on other business than usual …' Miguel's mother, she explained, regularly sold eggs to some of the better-off in Torre del Mar. But if she went in not to sell eggs then she had other business with the magistrate.

'The charges, you mean?'

'Yes, señor, that's what they say.'

'Well, we can only see what happens,' I replied and returned to my lunch. This isn't my business anymore, if it ever was. I need to finish writing; there isn't much left to say.)

11 September (cont'd)

On the way down to El Mayorazgo in the afternoons, there was the activity in the ravine to watch. Rising from nothing, where nothing had been, the dam slowly began to take shape, the gorge scraped and blasted clean. It gave me pleasure to watch the wall grow, the ease with which the two masons laid the irregular white stone as though it were brick. The men, ceaselessly mixing cement by hand, joked and laughed; and Bob – always Bob – directed things, working alongside them, to the men's astonishment at first. His building talk, during moments of rest, was often meaningless to me, but I appreciated it as I appreciated what was produced from the incessant labour below, as the concept, the structure from which this thing would be realized. Beside him, beside his practised experience, his boundless energy, my position seemed tenuous, but he never made any comment. There was satisfaction enough in the thought that one day the ravine would fill and the hills would burst into green. And then I would continue on down to the farmstead below.

It must have been early still, for the water was flowing when, in answer to some question perhaps, Miguel mentioned that for the past eight years, since his father's death, he had been responsible for the farmstead and his mother and sister. We were walking down the track to the cottage, I remember, he in front, and he turned, the exclamation or question stamped on his face, his eyes quite still, the suspended moment rapidly broken as he bent to fling a stone into the corn. I watched the sparrows rise, only to drop again somewhere. Yes, he had been only a year or two older than his sister was now, he'd worked alone until she could help, unable to hire a day-labourer since the señorita refused to pay a wage ...

'Señorita? But I always thought this land was yours.'

'Qué va! If it were ... All this is hers and that over there, and that as well, and the pasture hills ...' He pointed out the white farmsteads, El Vicente and Matanzas, beyond the watercourse, and to the hills beyond. 'And another farm on the other side of the road, there's the house there …' until it seemed that all the surrounding land belonged to her, with the exception of Bob's land above. Did no one farm their own land? Yes, there were some, there was Tío Bigote in the red-washed farmstead just beyond, hadn't I been there? He twisted an imaginary moustache to recall him for me, and I remembered the old man and the surprising red cottage, the colour of bull's blood, where once in a while I had found a carob's shade on the edge of the land. I laughed, imitating his gesture. Why did he paint the cottage red? A whim, Miguel said, a curious man. And that was true, for I remembered an afternoon when I came upon him irrigating and he strode over to where I stood watching, a tall, upright man with this big moustache, and more as a command than an invitation, told me to come. He took me to the edge of the terrace and showed me where the water flowed out, sparklingly fresh, from a borehole cut horizontally in the earth. 'Drink, drink!' he ordered, and I bent down and drank, exclaiming my praise, escaping as soon as I could for I had difficulty understanding his speech.

'His land is good, plenty of water,' Miguel said. 'Better than this.' With a growl he flung another stone and a flight of sparrows took off. 'They'll get the little that's left, they and the rats. And the señorita's half …'

Half to her? Of course, it was her land, half of everything went to her. Once a week she rode down on the donkey to fetch something he'd grown, to estimate the coming crops. Last summer she'd calculated sixty *fanegas* of wheat, but when he had threshed and the grain had been measured, there had been fifty-four. She had come herself and searched the farmstead, the attic, the cowshed. Before she did he had told her, if she found a kilo of wheat she could have the whole crop.

'And you put up with that sort of thing?'

'Ah! The half's better than nothing, isn't it?'

'All the same, there's a limit …'

A limit? Again that momentary look of silent exclamation. That was different, wasn't it? Because, in the years after the civil war, he remembered, when on top of everything else there'd been no water for three years, the people ate grass, weeds, anything they could lay their hands on. There was starvation then; even those with land only just got by.

And then he surprised me by suddenly laughing. 'The only egg we ate all year then was on Easter Sunday. My mother put one aside for each of us. The rest she had to sell. All year we waited for that day, we were so hungry. And for nothing. Our stomachs were so weak that as soon as we ate the egg we went behind the house and vomited it up. We were famished, I never thought it would end.'

Well at least things were better now, I said. 'Ah yes, for some, of course.' He wiped his forehead on the shirt-sleeve he always kept buttoned at the wrist. 'You couldn't go lower than in those years.' Then he walked on, his broad shoulders slightly bowed, and I noticed again coming from behind that it was impossible to be sure of his age. His head sat solidly, almost without neck, on his shoulders, and his stride seemed accustomed to a constant lifting of weight.

'How old were you then?'

'Ten, eleven,' he said.

'We must be roughly the same age then,' I replied, 'twenty-seven, twenty-eight.' He smiled agreement, and I felt his blue eyes on me wonderingly. His glance seemed then to be measuring a physical difference, the difference of strength and tread and resistance to sun. It lasted only a second, the time to make me aware. But when now I remember that full-eyed stare, I think he was not looking at me but at my condition: what was I doing, I who was free to live as I wanted, here in the hills? I who could sit in the square or the cafes of Torre del Mar watching the girls, what was I doing when I picked up his hoe and thumped it in the hard, dry earth? Or asked about water? Or looked at the olives? At best, I suppose, I might be like Bob; that would make sense of a sort to him. Otherwise I was a meaningless irruption into his world, a foreigner who appeared and as suddenly disappeared, who was outside the routine of the land and the turning of seasons as he was on the fringe of a world encompassed by the granary's mud-coloured walls ...

Was it that afternoon or another that I saw her for the first time close up – one afternoon, in the shade of the vine in front of the cottage, when Miguel gave me the water jar and I held it up as I'd seen him do, and the jet of water splashed over my face. Miguel threw back his head and laughed. A young woman, whom I'd only glimpsed in the distance, came out of the door and stared. 'Look,' Miguel said, and he picked up the jar, the water arching from the spout against the green of the vine and setting his Adam's apple bobbing on the flow. I tried again, choking. 'Fetch a glass, girl,' he said. 'There's no better water than this anywhere.' She held out the glass, waiting with eyes down until I returned it to her; somehow the water tasted less cool.

'I'll have to learn,' I said.

'Of course.' Under his curious expression there was a smile. 'Ana, fetch some chairs.' She went through the low door into the cottage where, following her, my eyes caught sight of a tintype on the wall: an insipid frizzed blonde trailing a rose against a background of a white ocean liner and blue sea. What dreams, I wondered, were contained in this vapid print? Ana was prettier, alive, real, I thought, as she returned with a rush chair in each hand. She went to sit on a brick bench built into the side of the cottage, where she picked up a sheet she was embroidering. From behind dark glasses I watched her, but her eyes never left the needle: she was motionlessly distant, impassive, her face high-cheekboned like Miguel's, darker, smaller, though, under a rim of black hair. Her eyes, too, were dark, nearly black.

I felt Miguel watching me, heard him say something about Bob and the dam. Yes, I replied, taking my eyes off Ana, it was going to be big, solve all the problems of irrigating at last.

'And the water?'

Ah, I replied, Bob had got it all worked out, and I explained his plans. 'It'll store a hundred million litres when it's finished.' I heard my voice rise so that Ana would hear. 'And the water is going to be for all these farms. You'll never go short again.'

But Ana didn't look up. 'The water's drying up,' he said.

'But there's still enough,' I answered confidently, 'and most of it is running to waste.'

He shrugged. From somewhere came the sound of a cow lowing, and Miguel's chair scraped. He said something to Ana and she looked up and pointed to the rocky slope surmounted by the pines. Without a word he got up, and I followed him. We went up the slope to where the two cows and the calf were tethered; it was on my way home.

As he loosened the rope from a rock, I asked if he made money from cattle. Fattening a calf, yes, he said; the cows were for ploughing. In bad years a calf was the only money he'd make. The señorita wanted him to fatten more but she wouldn't pay for a new shed. One couldn't keep livestock in bad conditions; but if he built a shed, it would remain her property. Again his eyes fixed in that stare which sometimes I think was a challenge to dispute what he said.

'And half of what you make on a calf would go to her anyway,' I said. There was nothing now to dispute. 'How much does El Mayorazgo make in a year?'

He told me down to the last centimo, referring to accounts which he kept, and it worked out at about three hundred pounds a year. But he didn't get even half. 'She won't pay for fodder or manure; the earth is worn out.' He untethered the calf and then suddenly turned; his face was twisted: 'You have to give too, you can't only take.' The words came out flat, almost half-spoken. Then the contorted expression returned to the usual open-eyed stare and I wondered if I hadn't been mistaken. I waited, but he said nothing more.

On the way up to the village I tried to imagine what it was like working twelve or more hours a day and knowing that six belonged to the landlord for the privilege of farming her land; better than nothing – and 'nothing' were those who stood in the square all day waiting for work – was that what it meant? And what then was 'something'? A plot of one's own? Everything was relative, depending on where one stood.

I walked up the last of the steep track, the sandals I had bought – like Miguel's ones – gripping the earth. Above me the village spiralled up to the fortress-like church on the top, a burnt ruin inside, its exterior unmarked. My thoughts turned to Ana, then unexpectedly went back: I remembered someone, perhaps Bob, telling me something I'd subsequently seen for myself: the higher up you went in those streets, the bigger, the wealthier the houses became. The richest, María Burgos among them, lived at the top. Below them, in cascading layers, you looked down on a scale until you reached the poorest day-labourers' houses on the bottom flank. Yes, I thought, that was what it was really about; and for the first time perhaps, looking back down the track, I saw not a landscape but the small farmsteads, the land itself.

9

I had another reason for going to El Mayorazgo now, and it's not one I've been ready to admit: the hope of seeing Ana. Sometimes she'd sit under the vine sewing, but more often than not she was inside the cottage or out somewhere with the cows, and I'd stay with Miguel on one of the terraces he was working. I caught glimpses of her more than I saw her; but when I did, her fine-boned face and dark eyes fascinated me. Or was it the impassivity of that face, the distance she kept? I longed to say something to her, but could never find the easy word, let alone the half-mocking, half-joking phrases that come so readily here. One of the young workers on the dam, I remember, called out something to her once as she passed on the track above and she, without stopping, answered something sharp that made all the men laugh. But when I was with Miguel she rarely spoke.

Except once, on an afternoon that comes vividly to mind now. Ana wasn't sitting in her place on the bench, nor did she come out of the house or from where I could see the cows tethered. She appeared unexpectedly on the track from the village. As she approached I felt Miguel looking at her and then, harsh and sudden, he swore. She raised her hand to her hair, stammering something. 'I told you, didn't I?' he said angrily.

'How do you want me to work with my hair in my eyes?' she answered sullenly.

'You're not one of those from the town,' he retorted, not looking at her.

'Ay! What do you think? Herding cows!'

'They look like men with their hair short, you can't tell the difference. Come here.'

She moved towards him. 'There's hardly any been cut, just where the ends die,' she protested. She turned round to him, her hair falling over her neck.

'The next time you do it, I'll hit you,' he said hoarsely.

Ana laughed. 'I'm not a child!'

'You've got beautiful hair. Go on, get up there and fetch the cows down.'

Ana went out into the sun where she stood for a moment, caught by the heat. Then, in her faded red skirt and black blouse that had seen too much drying in the sun, she started up the track between the terraces. Her brown legs carried her so easily that she seemed to float.

'It's the truth,' he shouted after her.

Suddenly, from a distance already, she turned and shouted back angrily: 'Save that for her,' and, with a shake of her head, continued up the track.

I didn't know what to make of this outburst, so violent and personal that I couldn't be certain I'd understood their Andalusian Spanish, which Miguel always spoke slowly to me. I waited in silence, watching her climb the hill and hearing her barren song echoing among the rocks. It was the only time I saw him in anger, lose control of himself. He didn't speak, nor did he ever refer to it again.

10

For several days I didn't go down; the scene remained in my mind, disturbing the tranquillity I went to the farmstead to find. But then the water dried up and everything changed. I found Miguel bent over the corn, the sickle flashing through the stems, the thin sheaves falling behind him on the dry earth.

'Hola! Out for a walk?' I caught an edge of derision in his tone, and said I'd come down to look at the dam: the retaining wall was already several metres high. 'Ah!' He took off his hat and wiped his face. 'They're still working then?' He knew the answer as well as I. Picking up the sickle he moved into the shade of the carob. 'Ay! The heat this year, I don't know ...'

His voice seemed drained, flat. I put it down to the reaping, the sun pressing down. Trying to rouse him, I said Bob had already put two miners to work on the new borehole; with a bit of luck the dam would still fill. He and all the farms would have plenty of water. One hundred million litres ...

'My brother had that idea ...' He bent down and I saw that the shirt was sticking to his back. The stone whirled across the terrace and fell with a crash in the corn. 'During the war: a reservoir – but it didn't come to anything.' For a moment, that full-eyed stare, questioning or exclaiming, I was never sure.

'But this is real,' I said. 'You've seen the retaining wall they're building.'

'Ah!'

From high up on the slope came the sound of cow-bells; Ana was bringing the cattle down. Miguel picked up his hook and began to reap again, the sheaves thrown from his arm with the regularity of a machine. He appeared to be going faster each minute as if to make up for wasted time, bent in the face of the sun which slanted over the western sierra, range upon range of shadow in the sky. Once, long before, I remember, I asked him if he had ever been to the sierra, and he laughed. He knew the mountains like the back of his hand, from the time when aged eleven or twelve, in the years of hunger, he had been a goatherd alone all summer with his uncle's herd. An undertone of loneliness, even fear – not so much of the work but of separation from the familiar land – lay in his voice as he talked of the sierra's vastness, his months in the company of a demented young goatherd encountered by chance, and the occasional uneasy acquaintanceship with a band of outlaws … Memories of loss and desolation that he preferred to elude finally by laughing them off.

But those were other times. Now he didn't laugh, looking up at the two cows and the calf coming slowly across the stubble, their bony flanks showing jagged. Ana was already by the cottage.

'Ah, it's time already.' He flung down the sickle and walked towards the house, past the terrace of tomatoes where the canes threw long shadows in the sun that was setting with a metallic glint.

When we were nearly past I noticed that the tomatoes were the colour of tobacco, the vines brittle. 'They're drying up,' I said, immediately struck by the futility of the words.

'They're finished.' This time he didn't stop, didn't look

round. I let him go on. The terrace of withering plants, which I had watched him carefully tie to the canes, irrigate, distressed me. Row upon row, the fruit already hanging in clusters, the crop was dying, the work going to waste. I looked at the furrows, the patterns drawn for the flow of water, which had turned powdery grey, dried out and useless, and an inertia settled on me. I summoned up anger to fight it. Miguel was sitting under the vine, staring at the tiles, Ana was by the low door. I stopped in front of him, but it was as much her I was addressing.

'The dam will mean forty or more hours of water for El Mayorazgo. Of the hundred million litres, you'll get at least one-fifth, twenty million litres. We've worked it out ...' Hadn't I calculated the amount with Bob, revelling in the figures, which seemed more real than the water itself?

'That much?' said Ana.

The old woman came out of the door, a black shadow, and stood beside Ana, staring.

'If the borehole strikes water soon, it'll fill up this summer. If not, it'll catch the winter rain.' I looked to Ana for approbation, felt her as though she were next to me.

But she paid no attention. 'There's hardly any fodder left, the calf will have to be sold,' she said harshly.

'Ay! Ay!' The old woman screeched.

An idea suddenly occurred to me. 'Why don't you sell the calf in Torre del Mar where there are plenty of foreigners? The price will be higher.'

Ana glanced at me, seemingly surprised. 'Yes,' she agreed. For the first time I felt she was openly acknowledging me. 'We can cut out the village middlemen, Miguel.'

Lost in thought, he didn't reply. Then: 'Ah! Ana, those apricots ...'

She looked at him; there was concern in her eyes, I thought. Without a word she picked up a basket and disappeared.

Tunnelling from a well was against the law. 'Can't anyone do anything about it?' I found myself asking.

'Hombre!' the tall miner exclaimed. I saw Miguel looking away as though dissociating himself from the conversation; the other miner was crumbling earth in his fingers.

'Well?'

The miner shrugged. A small village, he proffered, and I saw the doubt in his eyes. I glanced at Miguel, determined to impress him: 'There's the law, isn't there?'

The miner's mouth opened on yellowing teeth and he spat. 'How would the rich get fat if they didn't eat what belongs to others?' he said, pressing thumb and middle finger together in a gesture of carrying food to his mouth. The other laughed, but Miguel still looked at the ground.

'All the same …'

'Look,' the miner's exclamation pressed against me, 'tomorrow you need a permit, a bit of paper, a favour – work, and who do you go to? Nothing, no more than a day's work, a signature perhaps. What does it cost?' He turned to Miguel questioningly as though to ask if I understood.

'Yes,' Miguel frowned.

The second miner grinned. 'That's how it is. A small village like this, you keep quiet about what you know.'

'Look at his señorita,' Miguel's cousin went on. 'She wouldn't pay her share when they ran into difficulties digging this borehole.'

'He knows, Manolo, he knows,' Miguel muttered irritably.

'Well then, cousin, we'll show her when we hit water, eh?'

'It won't be for me,' he replied in the same voice.

'Vaya, Miguel!' He looked shocked. 'Don't lose heart.' The miners exchanged glances: they too must have heard about the señorita's plans to refuse to allow a channel across her land.

Quickly, to redress the balance, I exclaimed: 'There'll be water from the dam whatever the cost,' looking at Miguel, trying to catch his eye.

'There you are, cousin,' the miner laughed. 'Let the foreigners take over and we'll work for them. People like Sr Bob ...'

I felt a flow of confidence, ridiculous now, as I thought of everything Bob had achieved since that day by the empty hole in the square: days spent getting the farmers together, hours of bargaining in the back room of the bar, trips to Granada for the necessary permission. Though I had done nothing, the miners' regard for him seemed to extend to me.

'And they'll buy the land at a good price, like him,' said the other. 'Thirty pesetas a square metre. At that you'd be rich, Miguelito, eh?'

'It's not mine to sell. If it were ...,' and that quizzical expression hung on his face.

'But if she sells you'll get a share, it's the law. Not that you need it, you've got plenty put by.'

'Who, me? Me? Not a button, look!' Miguel made as if to turn out his pockets, obviously putting on an act that, expected or not, made the miners guffaw. A faint smile came to his lips.

Ah-ha shouted the men, stamping their boots, not in his pocket, ah no, but in the savings bank. They roared so hard I didn't catch the joke, which seemed to concern the land in some way. Then his cousin nudged me: 'Miguel's a rich man, did you know that?' and I saw Miguel's face caught in a stare that seemed to be signalling something I didn't understand. His cousin turned out his pocket. 'Full – full of holes,' he quipped. '*Qué me cago en diez*, one of these days the lottery will turn up.'

'And in a couple of months you'd be back where you are now,' said the other. 'The señorita keeps hers, she knows the trick. Buy some land, then you'll eat: tomatoes and cabbage like that skinflint.'

'Like her? You call that a life. They should have put her out of her misery when they had the chance.' I saw Miguel's face darken, and the miner saw too. 'Come, cousin, it's only a joke. That was the war, now we're all at peace, eh?'

Then the other turned to Miguel, saying he too had worked in her olive mill during the hunger years, he must remember. 'Half the minimum wage and never a bonus, eighteen hours a day, so she could get the oil out on the black market at night.'

'Yes, yes.' The impatience returned to Miguel's voice, as though he had heard it before.

'Come on,' said the cousin. The smoke had cleared. He tapped Miguel on the shoulder. 'Come and have a look.' He nodded to the tunnel.

'No, cousin, no …'

'Frightened then?'

'Ugh! Underground – no.'

'We'll all be underground soon enough as it is, eh?' Manolo laughed. 'Ah, don't worry, cousin, she'll change her mind when she sees the stream we're going to strike.'

'If God wills. Adió.' The intonation sounded like Ana's.

'If God wills or not,' said the other from the tunnel, but Miguel appeared not to hear.

I left him more cheerful than when we had come. The weight seemed to have lifted, at least so it appeared; but I never asked him to go to the borehole again, so I can't have been sure, can't have been, no. Alone I returned several times …

12

15 September

They knew it would take a month of tunnelling yet, even with the pneumatic drill that Bob got from somewhere. Though he hid it under his usual display of confidence, I could see his concern. He was in deeper than he'd bargained for when he started the dam; striking water was going to cost a lot more than he'd planned. Perhaps that was why, when we went one night to see María Burgos, he was less than his normal self. I had no such excuse.

I went in expecting a tyrant and found a small, pale, rather desiccated woman whom life seemed to have cheated, in the gloomy parlour behind the brass-studded door, which had opened a crack to show a wrinkled face I imagined was hers and shut with a slam to leave us waiting outside. Bob and I exchanged glances. But the face was a servant's and when María Burgos appeared in the parlour to which we'd been admitted finally, she contrasted with the sullen face that had refused us entry at first.

We sat on the uncomfortable upright chairs. Bob explained.

'Ah yes, water,' she said, sounding rather helpless, 'the water.' She breathed a deep sigh. 'The dam, yes,' she said, 'yes, of course …' and a look of weary anticipation came on her face; it was as though all the world came asking favours of her which, with a faint smile, she granted as best she could. She, a solitary woman in a world of men, she who had hoped the borehole could be dug, who had done what she could, but the farmers ...

Bob nodded appreciatively, knowing the mutual distrust, the unwillingness to pay, the quarrels he had pacified only by taking on the burden himself, by staking a large sum. A burden she, as a woman, had wearied of, deciding on a well with her cousin, the mayor, from which they hoped for water soon. 'With the cost, with the cost of everything nowadays, it didn't make sense to sink more money into the borehole. The people, you see ...' and her voice was confiding, soliciting agreement which we gave, in tacit understanding that, unlike the peasants, we could reach a civilized resolution.

But she committed herself to nothing – not that Bob asked for commitments, content, it seemed, to talk over the question, convinced that her interests were his. 'Ah, of course, of course,' she breathed. 'And with the coming of foreigners,' she smiled at her own delicacy, 'the land costs more. But the land – ah, the land doesn't produce more.'

Well, El Mayorazgo and her other farms would benefit soon, I put in, trying to give my voice the determination I sought.

Ah, of course, I knew the farm, sometimes went down that way, didn't I? The faint smile, her very best farm, the farm her father had entailed to her, hence the name, Inheritance. 'How productive it was in my father's time, but now ...' Her voice left a sense of disillusion in the air, an illusion of people's honesty shattered, of small reward for favours granted. After so much ... Then her voice took on an edge: the young no longer wanted to work as their fathers had done, they wanted something for nothing and if they couldn't get it they took it as though it were theirs. That wasn't the way. 'When I was young things were different,' and the edge was gone from her voice which now expressed sorrow, her eyes bewildered suspicion: the world she looked into, disappointed and dry, was a place of men threatening, cheating her of her rights. She had cause, her eyes seemed to say from across the dim room, fixing on mine.

Oh no, I protested to myself, not wanting to cause open disagreement when agreement was what mattered most. Miguel wasn't like that. But then the silenced assertion brought its own doubt: could I be sure? There were always two sides to everything, and the wheat – those missing *fanegas* he'd told me about ...

Her best farm, she repeated, which had prospered under old Alarcón, to whom her father had granted it when Miguel's sister was dying. Ah, she raised her hands in a deprecatory gesture that indicated this could be of little interest to us. What could one do, a woman alone?

Uninterested, concerned that she was forgetting or evading the reason for our coming, Bob returned the conversation to the water, the channel, the dam. He ran over the quantities of water to be stored, the hours of irrigating this would mean, the benefits for her farms: a glorious, if ill-defined promised land that moved his whole being as if in a dream, at which she smiled – indulgently, it seemed, reasonably, it seemed, saying only that she must have time to consider and would let us know soon.

Even now, to throw off the spell – though we knew we had achieved little – I have to remind myself of her acts, not her words. Though her words too, in throwing a shadow on Miguel, were destructive, it was her acts – or rather her inaction – that caused the greatest harm. Bob waited for an answer that didn't come, believing that when he struck water she'd see the immediate advantage of allowing a channel across her land. In retrospect, a terrible mistake.

It took nearly a month to hit water. Often, of an afternoon, I went to watch the miners at work. Their quick-witted irony saw through things, which to Miguel, in his circular routines, seemed closed. The local notables were a particular source of their gossip and I learnt much about the venalities by which they kept themselves in power. But when it came to politics, the miners clammed up: 'De política na',' they'd say, and it wasn't any easier to get them to talk about the civil war. Both had been youths then and claimed to have understood nothing of what was going on. They were prepared to talk about the chaos during the first days and their fear at seeing armed villagers patrolling the streets (one even with a sword he'd taken from a notable's house); they remembered the free distribution of food from the collective warehouse in the gutted church, and mass meetings in the square to elect village leaders. But the impression they gave was one of such disorganization that 'there was no way it could succeed.' We talked of many other things too, but never of Miguel.

One afternoon, crouched behind them in the low, narrow shaft, I watched the drill boring into the rocks. Suddenly it gave, the miners stumbled forward, jerked back; as the bit came out a jet of water shot from the hole as though from a punctured wineskin. I shouted, the miners grinned. More drill holes, more water pulsing with pressure. Miguel's cousin opened a cigarette case, took out three or four cigarettes, broke them open revealing a condom in each and, smiling, encased sticks of dynamite in them. He tamped the water-proofed dynamite into each hole, lit the fuses, and shouted 'Run!' Stooping, I ran the two hundred metres of blackness, the miners splashing behind, until, in the glare of the entrance, we heard the sharp crack followed by a rumble of rock.

The next day the church bell rang and the villagers poured out to see. By then the water was sweeping from the mouth, cascading onto the track from where it plunged into one of the many ravines that cut through the land, making a shimmering pool that overflowed uselessly between rocks and oleander while the land baked in the heat. At last María Burgos's answer came: 250,000 pesetas for the right to cross her land. Bob rejected it outright, intermediaries went back and forth, neither side moved. Immured in her house, she seemed indifferent to the fate of the land at her feet. Bob was angry.

'They want it both ways, want me to do everything for them and take me for a ride.'

The strain was beginning to tell. He'd expected her to give the right without payment in exchange for the water she'd get; now, she was asking not only a price, but a price so insultingly high that it was like a rebuff, Bob thought, a public blow to his good intentions.

Why did she do it? The punitive price was obviously meant to be rejected out of hand. It wasn't a question of money alone, therefore, and even less of striking a rational deal that would benefit her farms; no, it appeared she needed publicly to defy anyone who threatened her power and patronage as landlord. Everyone knew that her sharecroppers would soon be more dependent for their irrigation on Bob, who'd have the largest supply of water in Benalamar, than on her. But she could still show them who was the real power in the land, she could leave water to run to waste. As long as she continued to drag slender profits out of impoverished sharecroppers and soil, she would not bend before the power of an intruder's capital and his willingness to invest.

Bob retaliated, of course. He'd charge her 200,000 pesetas for the water for her farms. Stalemate. It went on like that for over three weeks. I kept out of it. I'd done what I could in loaning Bob a few hundred pounds I had spare for the cost of the borehole, a loan guaranteed by a plot of Bob's land that I could sell at a profit, so he said, once there was water. I'd even imagined building a small house, giving up the paper and living freelance.

But such dreams are gone. In those three weeks, it must have been, something broke in Miguel. And I don't know what it was because I didn't go down to El Mayorazgo any more.

13

No, in truth it had been even longer … As John leaned back in the chair, his head began to unmoor, drifting weightlessly. The ache which he had tried to ignore was now unmistakable. He got up unsteadily: Dolores was right, he ought to get out. He went into the bedroom where the smell of recently washed tiles and the pale light behind the closed shutters recalled, as always, a sub-aqueous world. With relief he lay on the bed, looking up at the tintype of Jesus he'd been meaning for months to remove, and tried to sleep.

Fitfully, his mind turned while his body cried out for rest. What was the point? Trying to recreate the Miguel he had known before anything else was known, trying to fix him on the page as though this activity were an end in itself. And what, finally, did he know of Miguel? The pages contained more about himself. All this lyrical activity was nothing but a stratagem, a ruse for tranquillizing the present, exorcising guilt, solidifying the past into a meaning. But there were other meanings he'd balked at. The truth, a simple little truth: Ana.

Instead of going to El Mayorazgo, he waited for her every afternoon on the track above the dam. Carrying a water jar, she had to go up every afternoon now, he discovered, to fetch water from the donkey man in the village. He waited for the faded red skirt to appear through the pines, waited to feel her brush past on the track.

She was inaccessible, unknowable, they never exchanged a word. Her face was more beautifully impassive than any woman's he had known. He could read nothing into it. What was she thinking? From the first afternoon at El Mayorazgo, John had sensed not indifference but an acute awareness of his presence. His skin tingled with it, his body came alive; the airwaves were full of uncertain messages: fascination, desire, danger. He watched her without letting her see, his eyes wandering over her body, her small breasts, brown legs. She knew, he was sure: messages came back from deep below her motionless face. He attracted her, but he'd have to do more, he was unknown, a foreigner. There was danger here. He never caught her looking at him.

In the shade of the pines he waited for her. Below in the gorge was the pretext for being in the same place each afternoon, the place where constantly he imagined tearing down the wall she put between them; imagining the instant of struggle, the collapse under the pines, the discovery of small brown breasts under his hand, so intimate now, under the sunwashed black blouse; smelling her sweat, dominating the inaccessible, penetrating the impenetrable, taking the unknown otherness for himself. He wanted her rapidly, wordlessly, the red skirt pulled up over her brown thighs; wanted to see her face break in passion, hear her long-drawn-out moan.

But as Ana approached, he always stepped back, away from the eyes that stared as though at a rock, an obstacle from which she moved with a harsh 'adió' drawn from the back of her throat, along the rim of the gorge. Once he followed her for a way, apologizing that he hadn't been down to El Mayorazgo for a while – how was Miguel? Without stopping, she replied that he was all right, and the tone of her voice told him to stay where he was: she couldn't be seen alone with him. And he watched her with longing as she started the climb in the sun, her hip protruding to take the water jar, her body barely moving under the skirt and the blouse stained with sweat under the arm hooked round the jar.

He knew why he wanted her: for the same reason that he pursued young working-class women in London. They were bodies for pleasure, born to serve, poor, screened by an invisible glass, and doubly dominated (he believed) by sex and that English thing he despised and yet used: class. Carried away, he took his pleasure, but afterwards inevitably felt a sense of despair.

It shamed him now to think that he could have wanted Ana like that. Miguel's sister! How often, too, he had wished that she, and not Dolores, had come to work for him! He was even more ashamed that he hadn't written the truth. For if she had come to see him that night instead of Miguel; if she'd said, the crops have dried up, there's no fodder left, Miguel needs a job on the dam, it's his only hope left of making enough to get through the rest of the year, John would have done anything she'd asked for, everything that was needed. Got Miguel a job on the dam, done it to impress her. Given her what she wanted in the hope …

John got off the bed. His head still ached and there was a bitter taste in his mouth. Below the window, children played hopscotch to the tune of 'Oh My Darling, Clementine' and the lottery-seller was calling his numbers. The cries went through his head. So, yes, that was the reason he hadn't done what was needed. A masturbatory fantasy had been more important to him than helping a friend. Here was self-interest more invidious and fatal for being kept secret than any Bob so willingly admitted to. He felt himself cheapened, the way he'd felt his friends were cheapened when, as soldiers in occupied

Germany, they'd bought a woman for a packet of cigarettes or a chocolate bar.

Gloomily he looked down at the stiff-legged children hopping, thinking of the months of self-examination, the piles of pages accumulated on the granary floor. Even as he was writing them he was deceiving himself! Taking refuge as always in the sly shuffling off of responsibility, letting it slip from his drooping shoulders as though the fit were too loose – no, nothing had changed.

In fact, he was shocked to realize, he'd done everything to ensure that nothing should change. Hunched over the tea leaves of his past, he'd justified his indifference to the present by the importance of understanding himself. The present, the afternoons with Miguel, had been a passing spectacle, a side show, compared to the passion of the morning task. Until the fateful flaws were uncovered there was no point in thinking of change.

One of the children caught sight of him at the window and pointed him out. John moved rapidly, closing the shutters, and sat at the table, his head in his hands, his narrowly constructed world beyond the point of repair. One might have expected that, as he surveyed the debris, his belief in writing as discovery and cure would have been swept away with the rest. But it survived and he clung to it. The method had been wrong but the means were right, he assured himself, determined to see his only form of expression survive the disaster. And there was proof! He had put aside the self-examination when guilt and despair had driven him to write about Miguel; and the unexpected result had been to reach a fresh awareness of himself.

Somewhere, in the direction he had unknowingly taken, he sensed a way forward. Stop picking at the scabs of his own past, as his mother would say (a blunt countrywoman whom he had never once surprised in a moment of introspection or heard utter a word of self-doubt); and live in the present. Perhaps.

The roar of Bob's motorbike outside shattered his thoughts – unmistakable because it was the only motorbike in the village. An ancient charcoal-burning taxi and the doctor's petrol-driven car made up the remainder of Benalamar's motorized fleet. For the rest – mail, foodstuffs, even water now – came by donkey or was carried on foot.

The bike's engine stopped and Bob came pounding up the stairs. The anger showed in his face as he appeared at the door. He thrust a piece of paper in John's hand: it was a summons to appear at the town hall. 'Jesus Christ! After all the trouble they've given me,' he exploded. 'They can stuff it.'

John was in no mood to sympathize with his anger. And moreover hadn't Bob got what he wanted in the end? A deal with María Burgos to channel the water across her land. It had cost him a lot, but not as much as she had originally asked. María Burgos had made her point, John supposed, had realized that it was detrimental to her power to go on being seen as the person mainly responsible for sending the hard-won water to waste. The agreement with Bob was designed to ensure that her power over her sharecroppers was in no way weakened; it was they who were going to have to pay for the water the farms used from the dam. Her own take for the right to cross her land she had kindly reduced to 100,000 pesetas. Even though this remained a scandalously large amount, Bob reckoned he would not, finally, be out of pocket: in a couple of years he'd get back from the sharecroppers the money he was paying in instalments to María Burgos. And he could now start, he was convinced, to sell plots through his Camden Town estate agency. That was why June, his wife, had gone back to London, he said, though John suspected there were other reasons, too.

When Bob told him of the deal, John had been too ill to take it in. Later, thinking of Miguel, he'd been angry: why had Bob let María Burgos get away with it again? He and John had already succumbed once to her person and forgotten the land-lord in her; and Miguel had paid with his life for that disastrous mistake. Now it was all her sharecroppers who were going to have to pay. Maybe, John thought hopefully, they would refuse. But then maybe, after all, it was better to have water, extra water that they wouldn't have had without Bob. Maybe ... And then he'd given way to his own feelings of guilt.

John glanced at the town hall summons in his hand. 'Why don't you tear it up?' he said. 'Forget it, forget these people, this place.'

Bob looked shocked. 'You can't be serious!' Despite all the set-backs, Bob's faith in Benalamar's future continued unshaken. John had often wondered why he didn't take his ideas to Torre del Mar on the coast where foreigners' houses were beginning to sprout: he was surely more likely to make a success there. But Torre del Mar was a run-down sort of place and the beach was grotty, Bob thought; Benalamar and its people, on the other hand, had an 'undefinable natural simplicity' that had touched his heart.

'Well, then, what are you going to do about it?' John waved the summons gloomily. Even before the answer came, he saw from the look in Bob's eye what it would be.

'I was thinking, would you mind going for me? Just to see what they're up to. You know what I mean?'

'Yes, I know what you mean.'

'You don't have to explain anything. Just say I couldn't make it, I had to go down to Torre del Mar.'

It was on the tip of John's tongue to say no when, begrudg-ingly, he replied: 'All right. When is it?'

'This evening at six. Thanks. I knew you wouldn't mind.'

14

There was still time enough before he had to go to the town hall. He had to get out, exercise his legs, which felt like a pair of old spindles. Think. As he put on his rope sandals, discoloured by earth and sweat, the memory of his past walks brought a flash of pain: but today he'd take a different path, explore something new.

The afternoon sun struck him in the face and for a moment he feared its weight, looking for shade, and finding a narrow strip beside the houses down which he walked like – it occurred to him – a soldier protecting himself from enemy fire. He laughed, pleased to see himself from the outside again. Instead of going through the square, he turned down a narrow street of day-labourers' houses that he usually avoided because people stared and once children ran after him, shouting and pointing as though he were some extra-terrestrial being.

Everything now was quiet, however, and the cobbled street between the low rows of white houses, which here and there incorporated live rock in their facades and formed odd angles (as though their builders had used the accidents of terrain to their profit), lay in the shade. The smell of cooking, rosemary and thyme mixed with rancid olive oil, filled the air. From a few doors away an old woman in black emerged into the street; the children were inside in the cool.

To his surprise the woman stopped in front of him, blocking his way. She lifted a hand towards his head.

'You're blond,' she said. Her fingers touched his eyebrows. 'A true blond.' Her crinkled face broke into a smile. 'It's not dye.'

'No, señora,' he laughed, 'it's real,' and he walked on, his good humour suddenly recovered, down the track, which started at the end of the street. In the sun again the air was sweating with heat, cicadas whistled in the olives, grasshoppers leapt with a flash of red wings. He ought to wear a hat, he reflected, then remembered that he hadn't owned one since that joyful day he turned in his National Service uniform. Well, he'd go back if he got too hot and tired.

Soon, indeed, John felt the sun heavy on his head and sat in the shade of an olive. Trying to remember where this track led, he followed its zigzagging course down from the village from where, already distantly, came children's cries and the dull clatter of the blacksmith's hammer. Suddenly it seemed to him that the path was a meaningless, insignificant trace trodden in the face of the rock, a thread of dust. The thing before it's known ... His sandals kicked at the earth; meaningless, unless one knew where it went, the purpose for its going, its end ...

Without his wanting it, the memory of Miguel returned on the edge of his vision. Blurred, uncentred. Seen like this, Miguel, too, was without meaning, like that first day slinging stones under the tree. To understand someone, he thought, you needed to see them at the centre of the picture, looking out at the world through their own eyes; see what they saw, the aims they set themselves, the hopes, ambiguities and resistances of their world: their meaning to themselves and to others ...

John shrugged. It was too late now, there was nothing to go on, he would have had to try to understand then. He thought back to that moment watching Miguel chasing off sparrows;

once explained, the purpose was clear enough, clear enough to take it as Miguel explained it, unquestioningly. But he'd never thought, he realized, to ask what the unspoken side of this action meant: the sort of life in which a man wastes himself scaring off birds all day from corn so thin you can see the earth between the stalks. Where a landlord takes half a man's work and water is scarce and allowed to waste, and a man kills himself for it.

John got up, it was time to be going back. He wanted to lie down for an hour before going to the town hall. Poverty, he thought, seeing the climb that awaited him and, at the same time, the figure of a man crouching in the shade of a tree on the track ahead. Half a dozen goats were feeding nearby. As he approached, he recognized the man: the sharecropper from Matanzas, one of the señorita's other farms, whom Miguel called Culebra, a nickname, John supposed, from the tongue flicked like an adder's from between his lips. It was he, John remembered, who had told Miguel that the señorita wasn't going to let the channel cross her land.

They exchanged a 'good afternoon' and John continued on his way, wondering why the sharecropper was this far from his farmstead. To find something to feed his goats, probably, he thought. He glanced back and saw Culebra, on his haunches, watching him. Then the old man got up and threw a stone at one of the animals that was gnawing an almond tree a few yards from where John stood.

'They poison the tree, it's in their mouths,' he shouted, walking towards John. 'They'll eat anything, they kill the trees.'

John nodded. He was about to walk on but the dark-skinned old face, a tangle of wrinkles spreading out from one that was more like a cut running from the edge of his eye to his unshaven chin, was already upon him.

'The land's lost this year,' he said, his tongue darting out between his thin lips.

'There'll be water when the channel's made up.'

The old man shook his head. It would come too late, there was nothing left to irrigate.

Bob had looked everywhere for piping, John knew, and suddenly there was none to be found. He'd decided instead to cut the channel by hand, a longer job because there was live rock to be blasted.

'If your señorita had more sense you'd have had water long ago,' John replied curtly. 'Look at what happened to Miguel.'

'Ay! Poor man. His betrothed threw him over. He said he was lost and killed himself for her.'

'And the water?' John tried to repress a mounting anger.

Culebra's lips pulled back over three stumps, chuckling. A man didn't kill himself because there was no water. 'If they did there'd be none of us left ... No, señor, two nights before he was all over the village looking for her. My nephew saw him, he was half mad already.'

The old man's certainty silenced John, who felt his eyes, hooded against the sun, watching him. Culebra bent down to pick up a stone, which he flung with a shout at one of the goats. Well, he thought, what was the point of arguing, it was over and done with. Then a flaw in the old man's certainty surfaced from the back of his mind: Miguel wasn't mad or half mad when he came to ask for work on the dam. Something happened after that, and that something was the señorita who made him go back on the deal ...

'Ah no, it wasn't like that,' the old man replied. He had been in the village when Miguel paid over the money for the calf. '"Here, look," says the señorita, "you've cheated yourself, fifty pesetas of this is yours." "My head's no good," says Miguel, "I can't add any more." She insisted and he took the money. "If there's no fodder for the calf, it's best to sell it now while it's still got some meat on it," she says. That's how it was.'

Confused and angry, John stared at Culebra's red-rimmed eyes. He didn't believe him, had never liked the look of the man. If that was the case, he said coldly, why had Miguel fetched the calf back?

'Who can tell what a man has in his head at a time like that? At sunrise on Wednesday, Miguelito went to my brother-in-law's house. "The deal's off," he says, and he gave him the money back. My brother-in-law needn't have let him have it, a man's word is his word, but he could see Miguelito was lost. It was the girl that bewitched him. He was crazy for her and she didn't want him; she went off to work for a foreigner on the coast. Ay! Women! A man keeps them down or they bury him, that's the truth.' Culebra bleated like one of his goats mounting another, his eyes moistening on the red rims.

A splinter of doubt pricked in John's mind. Could this be true? But if it was, if Miguel had handed over half the money to the señorita, how had he paid to get the calf back?

The old man's tongue flicked out. 'That's it, that's it, he was out of his mind. He must have repaid it out of his own money. He had money all right, there was no reason for him not to last out the drought.' El Mayorazgo always produced well, it was one of the señorita's best farms. He remembered her father, old Gil Burgos, terracing the land. In the bad years then, lots of people had emigrated, and those who stayed had to borrow to buy from his shop. When they couldn't repay, he took their farms, and so became owner of all this land. 'He knew a thing or two. And when the Reds came they found him in the village. He was too stubborn to hide, very stubborn he was. You see that rock down there, that's where they shot him.'

'Most likely,' suggested John, remembering his private fascination with the Spanish civil war at Cambridge, 'they were people whose land he had taken.'

'Na! They weren't from here, they came from Torre del Mar. It was like that then, these people didn't know what they were doing. No one in Benalamar would have shot him, he was respected too much. Even Miguel's brother, Antonio, made sure the señorita wasn't found.'

'Miguel's brother? What happened?' John tried to recall whether Miguel had mentioned a brother.

'He never gave away her hiding place, you see ...' The señorita had been hidden at El Mayorazgo by Miguel's father. Antonio knew she was there, of course. As head of the revolutionary militia he could have turned her in, but each time they went looking for her he was the one who ensured she wasn't found. 'A bunch of *granujas* they were, but Antonio was a good lad despite his ideas.'

'Did they look hard for her?'

'Of course. They searched Matanzas several times. The revolutionary committee was in charge. They took over all Gil Burgos's farms and half the crops, and we were working for them. *Granujas*, without discipline. At threshing time they came with guns for the share of the crop. One of them asked me how many hours a day I was working and I told them, "What do you think, from first light to dark." And he said there was no need, I wasn't working for a landlord any more, I could work half as hard.'

The old man took out a grey handkerchief and wiped his mouth. 'It only lasted six months and then our force came and all those bandits were shot over there in the same place by the rock.'

'And Antonio? What happened to him?'

'Escaped, never came back. Killed in the war, they say. Thank God, the señorita survived ... She was born to the land.' As a little girl, he remembered her accompanying her father to inspect the crops. She was his favourite and old Gil made sure she'd inherit the best of his land. 'And I'm grateful for it, she's always been good to us.'

John could take no more. As a parting shot, he asked the old man if he'd pay for extra water from the dam, as the señorita had agreed in her deal with Bob.

'Pay? Na! Once the channel's built there'll be water enough from the borehole. Na! Nobody needs a dam.'

III. The Search

15

His hopes of a rest gone, John hurried to the town hall, an old and beautiful building next to the square. Before going in through the thick double doors, flanked by a pair of sumptuous caryatids, he glanced again at the plaque embedded in the wall. Its celebration of Benalamar's Liberation from The Marxist Hordes by Franco's Imperial Crusade always repelled and fascinated him: like Medusa, the histrionic inscription seemed to petrify history with its vacant, triumphal eyes.

Smiling despite himself, he went into the whitewashed hall: Bob a Perseus, the dam a Pegasus risen from the Gorgon's blood? Not much chance, he thought, as a man in a shabby grey uniform asked what he wanted and told him to wait. He sat on a bench. No one else was about, the place was as somnolent as a graveyard. For three-quarters of an hour he waited for the uniformed man to return, falling at last into a somnolence of his own. The hurried return from the walk had tired him and he regretted being held up arguing with the old man down there.

His dozy thoughts took curious twists, coming from nowhere, overlapping, sliding sideways, vanishing almost before he had time to catch them. Fleeting figures, symbols: A→B→C→D, word plays … Enjoying the random glimpses, he made no attempt to think his thoughts, feeling at one with himself: flashes of nonsense – the chain of reason enchains – came and went in joyful abandon, connecting out of nowhere with: A:B:C:D ...

Roused at last by the grey uniform, forgetful of where he was, he wondered vaguely whether this was what Heine had meant about poetic inspiration: listening to an inner self and consciously rejecting nine-tenths of what flowed up. Or was it not Heine but another poet? The uniform pointed towards a closed door and John walked across: Pavese's phrase about the things before they were known, the things once known, ended with the words, *to become aware, to make history*. Why had he forgotten that? He knocked and a voice summoned him in. Expecting to find the mayor, he saw instead the town hall clerk, Ignacio, elderly, fretful, who rose from behind the desk and invited John to sit down. On the wall above hung a picture of the jowly Generalissimo and on another the languid profile of José Antonio, founder of the Falange.

John took the proffered seat. How incongruous it seemed, suddenly to be sitting in an office full of musty things, yellowing papers, stale conversations like overfull ashtrays when, outside, the land was scorched and water had still not reached the farms. Waiting for the droning voice to come to the point, which was being approached in loops of small talk, John observed Ignacio, head of a village administration of one. Rumpled black suit flecked with ash, black tie, an ancient typewriter – symbols of power: the ability to write, to fill in official forms, applications, the power of paying out old age pensions for which the fortunate recipients left him a tip. (Ignacio has to eat, the miners said; he gets only half a salary, graciously offered by the state-appointed clerk who left for urban pleasures many years ago, keeping the other half of his stipend and putting Ignacio in his place. No one wants to come here, no one wants to stay. *Pueblo perdido, perdido ...*)

Shifting position behind the desk, and with it the conversation, Ignacio casually referred to the dam and the water; just as casually, John expressed his regret that neither had anything to do with him. Ignacio's narrow face barely registered surprise. Raising his hand in a conciliatory gesture, he said it was regrettable that certain difficulties had arisen. For the good of the village, for all concerned. Naturally, everyone shared his concern, John replied.

The clerk's black eyes flickered over John's face, not unfriendly. 'There is a law, you understand, that enables such works whose usefulness is in the public interest to be taken over …' The phrase seemed to come from some yellowing tome.

'Ah, a dam for a life, perhaps.'

For once Ignacio looked taken aback. John recognized that the retort had been too sharp for anyone's good.

'Miguel Alarcón?' the clerk responded quietly, recovering himself. Yes. A tragic case, unfortunately not uncommon these days; in the past few years there had been at least two other cases, and in both of them the women concerned had been killed first. Then, returning to his subject, he added: 'Don Manolo, our mayor, would wish to use his good offices in everyone's best interest …'

'Yes, I see. Well, to be of use to the public the dam will first have to be completed and then to get water. There's still the channel to make …'

The clerk's dry laugh acknowledged the remark; for a moment the two seemed to be sharing a joke.

'But there is water. And the village, as you know, has none.'

'Ah yes.' John realized he'd been following the wrong track. 'Of course. But would there be any water at all had not considerable effort and investment been made?'

'Certainly, these things cost a lot of money. Such works as a dam, a borehole,' he said. 'In any case, I only wished you to know the position the law takes.' He paused; John was about to thank him and get up, when he continued: 'Sometimes it may be difficult for foreigners to understand our country. Did you know Spain before the civil war?'

John shook his head.

'No, you were too young, of course ... Well, much has changed since then. I often think that nowadays conflict and war are all one reads about in the papers. Last year the British and French with the Jews for the Suez Canal, then the Russians and Hungary. But none of these can equal in tragedy a civil war. Brothers fighting against each other, there is nothing worse.'

He sucked in his teeth and his eyes appeared far away.

'In your country there are many conflicts, many strikes, isn't it so? This is how it was here before the war. With you, the conflicts do not lead to war, but here ... The politicians were out for themselves, for power and fame, they didn't want peace.'

Where, John wondered, were these old man's ramblings leading? He leant back against the wooden frame of the chair. As clearly as though the words were written in the air above Ignacio's head, he saw what he had to do: find a different way to write about Miguel.

'Power and fame! Often I think of your Shakespeare, our Cervantes, writers who didn't seek publicity – men honoured only after their deaths. We are fortunate today because we have one man to honour in his lifetime, General Franco. Yes, there is a man who lives simply, who lives for Spain, who doesn't seek publicity.'

John expelled a deep breath. Almost automatically he turned his mind off the clerk's speech and let it take in his new idea, inhale it with deepening satisfaction: the sense of purpose that only a few hours earlier had lain shattered with the realization that he'd put fantasy above the reality of helping Miguel was partially restored. Now, he thought, I'll create a monument to Miguel.

Ignoring John's sigh, Ignacio continued: 'Before General Franco, there was never a stable government, all the time people were going round shooting each other. And then the Caudillo said *peace*, quiet, everyone get on with their own business and that's how it has been. Under him Spain won't fight wars. There aren't conflicts. Peace – that is Franco's genius, peace.'

Peace, thought John, having returned his mind to the clerk, peace in our time; whose peace, whose time? A dictator's peace, Miguel's peace. What he was going to write would be more like a war memorial than a tribute to peace.

'So it is his example we must follow, always seeking peace,' concluded the clerk, rising from his chair. As John made rapidly for the door, Ignacio added: 'In a small pueblo like this, it is always preferable to keep things among ourselves,' and John noted what he thought was a touch of complicity in his voice.

Smiling to himself, he walked with renewed confidence down the street. The explorer's passion that had locked him day after day in the granary flowed again through his veins. Fearful yet exhilarated, he saw himself forsaking the familiar yet uncertain terrain of his past – and a good thing, too! – to enter an unknown, uncentred maze in which, somewhere, lay hidden the flaw that had brought Miguel to destroy himself. If he could find it he'd weld the fragmented moments of a life into a coherent, living whole. It would be his tribute, his farewell salute to Miguel.

Carried away, his usual wary nature failed him at this point. The guilt and despair that had driven him in the past days to write about Miguel were genuine enough, even if they had produced little more than a nostalgic lament. But what could one say of the concept of a memorial, a farewell salute? For whom, in truth, was the tribute intended? For himself, of course! It was nothing other than a memorial to his guilt, repressed or sublimated in this apparently objective endeavour. But John remained serenely unaware of the deception he was practising on himself.

He stepped into the bar. Had someone mentioned the deception, had he indeed thought of it himself, he might well have replied: well, and how many other base emotions have provided the fertilizer for books, paintings, even music perhaps? But he'd have been on the defensive. As it was, the question that began to daunt him now was, How? How could he find out enough about Miguel to write such a tribute?

The bar was full of labourers, standing, talking, playing dominoes at drinkless tables. At the counter he found three or four of the men from the dam among the few who had money for a drink. They hadn't seen Bob all day, they said, inviting him to a beer. John declined with thanks and went up to Bob's house. It was in darkness, the motorbike not parked in its usual place, and he returned leisurely to the square and sat on a step by the dry fountain.

A great harvest moon was climbing up the sky, silvering the white walls. One would have to gather every sort of possible fact about Miguel's life, he thought, about his childhood, adolescence, the years after his father's death when he farmed El Mayorazgo alone – and these past months. He'd have to start questioning people, like a reporter, because there were no other apparent sources. For a moment he cursed his bad luck at never having been a reporter – a police reporter especially – instead of a sub-editor and leader writer. But he could learn.

Across the square, at a table outside the bar, he noticed the usual quartet taking the evening air: Don Manolo, the doctor, the falangist trade union chief and the baker, who doubled as justice of the peace. Two people, the priest and the sergeant of the Guardia Civil, were missing from this group, which ran village affairs, but then neither usually joined the others at the bar.

The square at this time in the evening was exclusively male; only on Sunday evenings did it fill with couples in a slow, endless promenade round its narrow confines. Rich and poor, old and young, girls arm in arm, ogling young men, children – all in their Sunday best – showed themselves off. For a couple of hours they circled on themselves, enclosed like the village itself in a world of its own. Beyond these walls nothing else seemed to exist.

The village was the centre of their world. A number, John knew, walked or rode occasionally to Torre del Mar; very few ever got as far as the town. Every evening, when he could, Miguel, like the other small farmers, came up to the village. It wasn't hard to imagine, after all, that this was the closest to urban life, urbanity, that most of them would ever know. It needed a leap of the imagination, however, to feel what it meant.

To his surprise, the flashes of nonsense which had come from nowhere while he waited in the town hall suddenly seemed to make sense. His attempt to understand Miguel's death had been focused solely on cause and effect: A→B→C. The chain of linear reasoning was false. It had made his suicide appear a fatality, 'explained' by events, when in fact, it was in the way Miguel lived this constellation of events (A:B:C) that the fatal flaw could be found. Was it possible to discover something like that – how, inside himself, he'd lived things? And who would know – for sure, that is? His mother? Ana? Perhaps, but his mother wasn't going to talk, and Ana …!

John looked at the moon nailed above the rooftops, its light making the square appear even smaller. He'd sat here many more evenings than Dolores knew, enjoying the English char-acteristic of seeing without being seen. From now on asking questions without appearing to ask them was going to be his task, so that his enquiries didn't anger or scare people off. It was no business of his, was it, to be stirring things up in a place that lived under the Pax Generalissima.

At that moment, out of the corner of his eye, he saw the simpleton's white raincoat across the square and heard the words, 'Santa María, pray for us ... Santa María ...' and remembered that on nights of full moon the man often took himself for a priest and preached sermons from the rock. Then he'd come down to the square and pace back and forth, imitating the priest: twelve paces this way, twelve paces back, for hours on end, without anyone taking any notice.

He was, people said, a cousin of María Burgos, though his narrow Mexican-Indian face seemed to belie it. From the miners' stories, John knew of the more spectacular venalities of the people sitting at the table across the square. In his private practice the doctor received (thanks to the mayor's munificence) the salaries of the two state doctors who had been unwilling to stay in Benalamar. During a typhoid epidemic, he'd charged ignorant peasants for inoculations that were free; and when he bought himself the first automobile to be owned in the village, it was quickly dubbed with that ready wit of the Andalusian poor, 'the people's car'.

But the priest, Don Salvador (who never deigned to speak to foreigners or to most of his parishioners either as he paced up and down the square in a cassock reading his breviary), had obliged the doctor to return the money. As for the mayor, everyone knew that beneath the 'Don' lay the village noodle-maker of his youth and the black marketeer of the hunger years, who sold the rationed flour he was supposed to distribute and invested his illicit gains in farmsteads let out for sharecropping.

Just then the simpleton stopped in front of the table and began waving his arms. What was he doing, begging? But there were no beggars here; John remembered having asked Miguel once and he had laughed: who would there be to beg from in Benalamar? No, it was more like a sermon the simpleton was giving. The doctor told him off loudly, but he didn't move. The mayor, his heavy head sunk in the neck of the pyjama top he was wearing, got up and walked away silently. Men's faces appeared at the window of the bar. The simpleton resumed his pacing. It was probably a family affair, thought John.

But the white raincoat suddenly stopped again, the arms waving like a mechanical saint's. The doctor shouted. Plain and clear came the simpleton's voice: 'Confess, confess the sin of taking from the poor. Renounce thy car paid for by the people, thou ...'

Shrugging, trying to grin, the doctor got up and followed the mayor. The simpleton was saying the things that everyone knew but that the miners said couldn't be said. A mad prosecutor, flapping his arms, bowing his head, pacing again, oblivious of the eyes fastened on him. The union boss got up casually and, as casually, walked out of the square. The baker didn't move quickly enough: the simpleton stopped in front of him and, reaching into his raincoat, pulled out what looked like a revolver.

'And thou for thy murders...!'

'No!' cried the baker. But men from the bar had already grabbed the hand, and there was a shout, then guffaws. They raised the revolver and John saw it was a large key.

White in the face, the baker slunk away, while the impossible raincoat resumed its pacing. John was laughing to himself when the rustle of a black cassock almost brushed his face. The white-coated arms went up in what looked like readiness to embrace the priest, but instead the simpleton's high-pitched voice cried: 'Hypocrite!'

'Get inside,' the priest ordered.

'Hypocrite! Thou who refuse burial to the poor.'

'Get inside immediately,' the priest hissed, brushing past the uplifted arms.

'Thou hast betrayed the word.'

'Desgraciado!'

'The word. The wor–' Eyes sightless, he was standing staring at John. Then twice, very clearly, he repeated, 'the bell ...' and turned away to resume his pacing, in silence now.

The bar was full of men still laughing as John passed them on his way home. A pleasant anticipation warmed him as he thought of tomorrow. A new start always gave him a heady feeling. Who knew where it would lead, what it would produce? Perhaps even things (as a mere by-product, of course) about himself, as writing about Miguel had already done.

16

Bent over the stove preparing breakfast, Dolores didn't hear John come in, and she jumped, smoothing down her faded blue dress, her eyes as startled as a hare's.

'Did you want your coffee? It'll be ready in a minute.' She put a hand to her hair.

'That's all right, there's no hurry.'

She saw he was smiling, his eyes bright. She wondered what he was doing in the kitchen where he'd only been once or twice and never this early. His presence surprised her all the more because, since he'd returned to the granary in these last days, he'd become distant again, as though absorbed in himself.

'Do you know what happened last night in the square?' he said, launching into an account of what he'd seen. Dolores nodded: everyone in the village knew, she'd heard about it from a neighbour before going to bed. 'So is it only the mad who can tell the truth here?' he laughed.

'Your coffee is ready. I'll bring it to you.'

But no, he'd have it in the kitchen, he said unexpectedly, and sat down at the table. There was another chair and he asked her to sit down and have her breakfast. Taken aback, Dolores shook her head: thank you, but she had hers later. She remained standing by the stove, unsure what to make of this turn of events.

John, evidently, was determined to chat. It made a pleasant change, she thought; he was looking well again, his face was newly sunburnt so he must have gone out. She'd guessed right, because he started to tell her he'd taken her advice and gone for a walk yesterday afternoon and met Culebra by chance.

Dolores listened to John's account, not wanting to say anything. There were many things better not spoken of, especially to a foreigner, and she remembered that she might have said too much in the past. One shouldn't talk about politics – 'de política na', it was dangerous – and she'd managed not to say anything about the simpleton. But Culebra's story angered her. Still she said nothing.

John observed her silence and went on talking, confiding in her about his conversation with Ignacio, the town hall clerk. He laughed as he described the scene in the dusty office and the clerk's disquisition on peace. Then he recalled his fascinated horror at the plaque on the town hall wall. 'Marxist Hordes,' he repeated, 'Imperial Crusade.' And he told her how at Cambridge a tutor's remark, tossed off with customary arrogance, that the wartime Republic had been nothing but a Communist front, set him to reading. (The civil war, of course, was too contemporary an event to have figured in the degree.) For a term or two his fascination with the war, which he remembered distantly from his childhood led him to learn enough Spanish to read some of the memoirs and reportage in the original; but then, under pressure of exams, the interest withered and he hadn't returned to the subject.

Dolores remained by the stove, nodding occasionally but bewildered as to the purpose of this unexpected talk. Against her will, she found herself lulled into an intimacy closer than when he'd been ill. He seemed to be offering something she couldn't return. To ease her mind, she broke more brushwood across her knee and put it into the stove, and when she turned round John was sitting with his eyes half closed and in silence. She waited for him to speak again, but he said nothing. For minutes that seemed like hours he sat, half looking at her. She shuffled, thought of asking if he wanted more coffee, but couldn't bring herself to speak. Momentarily she wondered if he was ill again, but she knew it wasn't that. There was nothing but his silence. It entered her with the power of an alien dream, overwhelming her with the urge to break its hold. She was as frightened of silence as most of us are.

'Culebra, what does he know?'

She had to shake herself free of the fear. And then came the questions, one after another, soft-spoken and unremitting, while he sat there motionless, his eyes fixed on hers. Before long, she found herself turning away to dab at her eyes; then at last, to her shame, she burst into tears.

17

16 September

Dolores said: 'Culebra, what does he know? He wants to put all the blame on Miguel's betrothed because he has his relations with the señorita to mind. She and he are as close as these two fingers of mine. She got him off after he slashed the sharecropper at El Vicente across the neck with a hoe and sent him to hospital for several months. It was a wonder he didn't die. Culebra was stealing his water and the other man came to protest. No, you can't take Culebra's word for anything, everyone knows that. And in any case, if Juana were to blame, more likely Miguel would have killed her first, don't you think?'

'Um...!'

It had happened a couple of times before, she continued, but Miguel hadn't laid a hand on Juana as far as she knew. True, they'd quarrelled, but what couple didn't when they were betrothed?

'What did they quarrel about?'

'People said it was because she went down to the coast to work and Miguel wanted her back. But I don't know, people say all sorts of things like – like that she was seen talking to a man down there, that sort of thing.'

'So what Culebra said was true. Who is she?'

'Juana Moréno.' No, the reason people blamed her was that she was betrothed before and threw over her novio. 'That's not in her favour, is it? The men say, you see the sort of girl she is, what can you expect of her, but it's not her they ought to blame, it's not her fault, she –'

'What's Juana like?'

'Like? Well, dark, about my height, quite pretty.'

'I mean as a person.'

'Oh. Gay, I suppose, yes, not that she's got anything to be gay about now.' For several years when she was little more than a child Juana had worked in the bakery next to Dolores's house to help out her widowed mother who had nothing. Juana had always seemed cheerful despite the hardships.

'Were they planning to get married soon?'

She didn't think so. Miguel hadn't bought the furniture; he probably wasn't thinking of getting married for two or three years. 'He wasn't like most of the men, was he? Because, although he had the farmstead, he had his mother and sister to support, he had to think of them first.'

What had happened to Juana's father, I asked.

For a long instant Dolores didn't reply. She looked out of the window as though, I thought, to see if anyone was passing. Then, in a whisper, she said he'd been shot.

One of the leading militants of the anarcho-syndicalist CNT, he was too ill to flee when the village fell. The local falangists dragged him out of bed and shot him with a dozen others.

'The people here shot a number of landlords, didn't they?'

'Some people who called themselves anarchists came from Torre del Mar to clean up the village. We were sheltering falangistas, they said. The first time Antonio managed to get them to leave, but they came back again when he wasn't here.'

'Antonio?' I said.

'Yes. Didn't Miguel tell you? My betrothed, his brother.'

'Your betrothed! Go on.'

'He was only eighteen when he had to flee the village. We'd been engaged seven months.'

'What did he do that he had to leave?'

'Nothing, nothing,' she cried. 'But he'd have been shot if he'd stayed. It was the saddest day of my life, seeing him go. And yet I knew he had to.' She turned and lifted her apron to dab away a tear, hoping I wouldn't see.

I said: 'Let's start from the beginning. I want to get this straight.'

Little by little her account began to come clear. Antonio was the eldest son, twelve years older than Miguel. Against his father's strong opposition, he joined the Libertarian Youth in his teens. Dolores became a member eighteen months later. From the start, she liked this cheerful, joking youth who even then seemed to take nothing for granted. There were many young girls who had their eye on him by the time he had to go out day-labouring because El Mayorazgo couldn't provide work for two pairs of hands. Much of the time he was out of work or on strike. The landlords pulled up their vines, telling the labourers *their* Republic could feed them. Antonio led the labourers into the vineyards. She watched him growing in militancy – he was a member of the CNT now – and stature; he saw everything so clearly.

One day he stopped her in the street. 'This evening we'll walk out,' he said just like that.

'Oh! What makes you so sure?'

'Because you're the one I want.'

'And supposing you're not the one I want?' she'd replied. But the flush that came to her cheeks told them both she was lying. They walked out together that evening; a year later, just before the war, they were betrothed.

It lasted only a few months. 'I knew happiness once and I shall never know it again.'

She broke down sobbing, her face hidden in her apron, the sound of Antonio's name repeated again and again. Unresisting, she sat on the chair I held out for her. For a moment I laid a hand on her shaking shoulders, then thought better of it.

18

Later

My silence this time gave her a space and the time to relive her sadness. At last, wiping away the tears, she said she was sorry she'd cried, she hadn't wanted to. She got up and stirred the embers in the stove and put on more brushwood. The smell of rosemary and sage filled the kitchen. After a time she brought the coffee pot to the table and poured us each a glass. The goats' milk tasted creamy and sour.

Then in a low voice she said: 'Antonio was one of the last to leave the village before it fell; he knew his fate if he stayed.' For days and days she had cried, it was the end of her world. During the civil war she'd had two letters from him, via the Red Cross, but it was only at the end of the war that she learnt he'd been killed on the Ebro. He never gave up his ideals, he believed in the revolution until the end.

How had he reacted to the start of the military uprising, I asked.

By then he was one of the CNT's leading militants in Benalamar, she said. He was among those who attacked and reduced the Guardia Civil barracks. When the guards came out with their hands up, one of the attackers shot the sergeant dead. Antonio knocked the shotgun out of his companion's hand. 'If you want to kill fascists, go and kill them in open combat,' he shouted, but it was too late.

'He had always been against killing; he believed the land-owners' land should be taken but not their lives. "What's the reason for sending them up there," he pointed towards the sky, "when they can learn to work down here for the first time in their lives?" The land must be for those who work it, not for those who own it. The labourers should take over all the land and work it collectively. How often he said to me: "That's the only way we can control our own lives, ensure that what we produce remains ours to deal with for the good of all. But not egoistically, like the bourgeois. No!"'

'Did he make it work?'

'He helped to organize a collective on the big estates in the plain. All the produce was distributed free in the village, so much per head. We felt such joy: the revolution had happened! We were free, no one had to work for anyone else, when you went out to till the collective's land you weren't thinking of the cacique or boss.

'But Antonio couldn't do anything with the sharecrop-pers. He tried to persuade his father that he'd be better off if all the sharecroppers put their land together, worked together. "Look," he told him, "we'll get mechanical threshers so you don't have to thresh by hand any more, we'll have one cowherd and a new cowshed so each of you doesn't have to waste time, we'll cement the irrigation channels … And half the produce won't go to the landlord any more."

'But his father wouldn't listen. He believed in the old ways. As a young man he had served the Burgos family; he and María were the same age. Antonio told me she'd wanted to marry him, but he turned her down. For a long time his father didn't speak to him.'

'Did he ever mention the collective building a dam?'

'I don't remember. Perhaps. He was full of ideas, always thinking of something new, of the future. But it only lasted six months here, there wasn't time ...'

And his father had hidden María Burgos?

Yes, it was true, though Antonio had never said anything even to Dolores. She found out only when the Franquista military took the village and suddenly the señorita reappeared. She'd escaped in the first days when some of the extremist youth were looking to round up the landlords. That's when they set fire to the church ... María Burgos got out of her house at night dressed as a man and escaped to El Mayorazgo. The old man had a hiding place ready for her underneath the cowshed.

'So it was all prepared?'

Dolores nodded. 'There was great hatred among the labourers for the landowners. It got even worse just before the war when the owners boycotted the workers. So the señorita must have known what was coming ... Antonio always kept the revolutionary militia away from El Mayorazgo.

'He saved her life,' I exclaimed. 'He could have turned her in.'

'Yes,' she said. 'At the end of the war the señorita put in charges against him. He would have been shot if he'd come back. They shot so many, ten times as many as the landlords who were killed. The crucifix and the rifle, they said, but it was the rifle they used. If he had to die, I'm glad he died fighting the enemy face to face.'

19

16 September, evening

Dolores was worn out, her face drawn and flushed from crying. I still had many questions in my mind. Miguel, his mother and father, the señorita ... For a moment I thought of pushing her further, then decided against.

'You're tired. Let's leave it there for now. This afternoon we'll talk some more.'

She nodded. 'I must go to the market to buy lunch. I don't know if the fish vendors have come.'

'Get whatever you can,' I said, and went up to the granary. I wanted to write down the conversation as accurately as I could before I forgot. Her hatred of María Burgos had solid reasons, I now saw, and it would have to be taken into account in anything she said. Was this perhaps why she refused to give real credence to the idea of the quarrel between Miguel and Juana?

In the afternoon we sat in the kitchen again. She seemed more relaxed, as though the worst had past. The heat came through the open window in waves deflected from the walls across the narrow street which was silent in the somnolent after-lunch hour ...

'Tell me about Miguel's father,' I said.

'What was there to tell?' she replied. He was one of the old sort, he'd had his own herd of goats until Carmela, Antonio and Miguel's sister, fell ill, and he'd had to sell the herd to pay for medicines. She died and he was left without anything. He went to see the señorita's father, old Gil, in his cloth shop. The sharecropper at El Mayorazgo had just died too, and he, who had never asked a favour in his life, now asked Gil the favour of his life. For the first time anyone could remember, indoors or out, he took off his hat. If he didn't get to his knees it was because for no one in this world or the next had he ever fallen so low. Removing his hat was a sign not of deference but respect for a peer. He uttered his request in a few, plain words, as was his custom, and without explanation or justification. Austere, self-contained, he looked Gil straight in the eye. No one was certain whether Gil knew that his daughter had wanted to marry him once; nor why he granted the favour when there were so many others he could have chosen instead of a goatherd down on his luck.

Once, in his presence, Dolores recalled, Antonio attacked the landlords who were refusing the labourers work. His father rose from the table. 'You've brought it on yourselves, this is a Republic of disorder. I've known worse times and you may yet, too. Go and join your own.' Antonio got up and left. 'He'd been disrespectful, one should never argue with one's father.'

'Was he harder than most?'

She didn't know about most, but he was much harder than her own father, for example, who'd always been loving to his children.

'And the mother?'

'Very devout – but a warm, loving woman whom Antonio worshipped. A real countrywoman who could carry seven sheaves of wheat from the farthest terrace to the threshing ring. "She had to work hard, much too hard, at El Mayorazgo when I was small," Antonio had said. "Ana was almost born in the fields." He never wanted to see a woman have to work like that again.'

'When Miguel was Antonio's age, did he have the same sort of character?' I asked.

'It's possible,' Dolores replied. 'But Miguel was more – how shall I say – the more withdrawn of the two, you could never be sure what he was thinking. Antonio was more of a fighter, he wouldn't have done what Miguel did. He would have told María Burgos what he thought, the way he told any landlord when there was trouble. But I didn't know Miguel the way I knew Antonio. He was only young then. I remember during the hunger years when his father sent him as a goatherd to his uncle in the mountains, a terrible thing happened. Miguel – he was only eleven or twelve – came down from the mountains and found his uncle had been killed by the outlaws; people said they suspected he had informed on them. Imagine it! Terrible! Coming into the house to find the outlaws still there and his uncle dead. Poor child, I remember when his father fetched him back, his hair was hanging to his shoulders and he looked like something wild. Alone in the mountains with those goats, and the outlaws – even in times as bad as that a child shouldn't be sent to the sierra. His father could have found him something here. But that was how the father was.'

'I told you what Culebra said, that the señorita didn't make Miguel go back on the deal. Why do you say she did?'

'Because I know!'

'How?'

'Her servant told me. She was standing outside the door. The señorita gave him back the fifty pesetas he'd added up wrong. Then she said, "You can cheat yourself, but don't try to cheat me. Fetch the calf back, I didn't say you could sell it." She called him a lot of bad names, and he went out the door as white in the face as if he were already dead.'

Neither of us said anything. Her eyes were shining with tears of rage – and triumph too – and the silence belonged to her.

In the square, the past hung heavier than the present with its familiar street sights. Returning donkeys, a flock of goats being driven into a house, the men coming in bowed under the weight of firewood – the eternal evening scene – appeared suddenly with the unreality of a stage set onto which he'd walked from the hidden workings backstage. John looked at the men and saw each with his own history within him, unspoken, silenced perhaps. That old man standing against the wall had lived through a revolution and civil war, barbarous shootings, hunger years; what did he, who would never appear in history books, have to tell? Or that middle-aged labourer who must have been only a child then?

They could, if they wished, tell what it felt like, the intimate taste of hope and despair. They'd survived. And then John realized how little he still knew about Miguel. Dolores had left him with one incisive memory, but that was of Juan Alarcón's younger boy, the little brother of her beloved Antonio. He needed to find someone who had known Miguel well.

John was already closer than he suspected. Later, as he lay resting, he shuffled and reshuffled the memories of his conversations with Miguel. Then, for the first time, it seemed, he noticed a name that repeated – but for which, unusually, he had no association. Pepe … Pepe … familiar, freely named, just unknown to him. With sudden energy, he rose and left the house, heading towards the bar. 'Juanico will know!'

Pepe el Conejero. The barman knew him, of course, and agreed to arrange a meeting. In the bar the next evening, John found a young man with a slender, open face, confident brown eyes and a firm handshake. He didn't remember seeing him before, though Pepe said he worked on the dam; but then it was a long time since John had been down to the site. Opposite Pepe sat Cristobal whom John knew well by sight, for he was the man who called to Ana in the afternoons when she walked by on the track above the gorge, and he'd envied the ease of his flirtation with her.

Until a few weeks ago, Pepe had sharecropped a farmstead beyond El Mayorazgo in the hills. This year was the worst he had known in eleven years of sharecropping. He'd arranged to sell his last calf a month ago down on the coast when the farmstead's owner, Culito, said no, the calf wasn't to go.

'We were standing in there at the bar, I gave the counter a bang with my fist, so hard all the glasses shook. "The calf's going tomorrow because I've made the deal." He knew what I meant. Last year he lost me two thousand pesetas by holding out for more when I'd made the deal. He didn't say anything, he could see I was serious. Later Juanico asked how I could be so disrespectful to the landowner and I told him I'd do the same to anyone except my father whom I respect.'

Pepe's face, which had resisted the furrowed immobility of the men in the square, registered disgust. A month ago he'd gone to ask Bob's foreman for work on the dam. 'If it wasn't for Sr Bob I don't know where I'd be. The landlords here see the people in the bar and they say, "The sharecroppers are cheating us, they must be if they've got a *duro* to spend." They don't want a man to live.'

It wasn't like this in Torre del Mar where the people owned their own land, put in Cristobal. Pepe nodded: there a man could live like a human, take a day off now and then, go to the town.

The moment had come; looking at Pepe, John spoke quietly.

The señorita? Of course she was worse, Pepe replied, she was richer. 'If it had been me I'd have told her what to do. Once a man has given his word on a deal, win or lose, he doesn't go back on it. Miguel was like that – only he never talked back to her, he had too much respect. He went out of her door and a friend – Pedrico, it was – called to him to have a coffee. "I don't want any," he said, and he was white in the face. Pedrico had never seen him like that.'

A question came to John out of the blue. Could she have objected to his selling the calf to Tío Bigote?

Pepe looked dubious. In the past, Miguel and he had always sold their calves in the village. But this time Miguel must have seen he could get as good a price from his neighbour. 'Miguel always worked everything out, he struck better bargains than any of us. He made a lot of money because he was the best farmer around here …' He'd plant an early crop of maize, the same with tomatoes – last year he'd made ten thousand pesetas for his early tomatoes; a lorry came specially from Granada to collect them. Imagine that! No one here had ever done anything like it before. 'Miguel noted down all his expenses, he kept accounts, not like the rest of us; he even noted down the date he crossed a cow.

'Everything came easy to him. I remember last year when he was irrigating at night he'd turn the water into the alfalfa, jump on his bicycle and ride up to see his *novia*, then he'd come pelting down to change the water to another terrace and ride up again. And when I shouted, "Are you irrigating, Miguel?" he shouted down from above, "Yes, I'm irrigating from up here, look!"'

Pepe's face broke into a smile at the memory. Miguel had been happy and carefree then.

'So what changed?'

'Miguel took the quarrel with his betrothed badly, that was the truth,' Pepe replied. 'It was just a tiff, the sort of thing that happens to everyone, but one night a month or so ago, on their way down the track together, Miguel said: "Pepe, I'm lost ..."'

Pepe told him not to be foolish. '"We're all lost," I said. I'd heard something of the quarrel, but a man doesn't take that sort of thing to heart.'

'He shouldn't have let her go down to the coast, that was the start of the trouble,' put in Cristobal sharply. Someone had seen her wearing trousers in the foreigner's garden. 'In trousers, yes. If Miguel had known.'

'Trousers?' John asked.

'Yes. Trousers are for men, aren't they? And not only that, she rode the foreigner's horse on the beach and swam in the pool. It was becoming a scandal, people in the village were beginning to talk. That was when her mother went to fetch her back.'

Walking up from the coast, Juana and her mother had stopped at El Mayorazgo for a drink of water. Miguel was there. He and Juana had had a fight the weekend before about her cutting her hair. 'Juana shouldn't have gone to see him. It's not the custom, a *novia* doesn't go to see a man when they've quarrelled, eh Pepe?'

Pepe nodded. 'Yes, Miguel was angry because she had had her hair cut like a foreign woman.'

John smiled to himself, and then the memory returned of Ana coming down the track and Miguel's anger over her hair.

'Who does Juana work for?'

'They say he's a marquis or a lord, he was at the fiesta Sr Bob gave at the dam. A tall man with a moustache ...'

Lord Bughleigh, of course, staggering up on rubber legs to declaim Dante in Italian – who could forget it? He stood on a chair, swaying, never missing a line and without his usual stammer. The cheers at the end united for the first time the separate worlds of the dam workers and the foreigners up from the coast for the event, none of whom had understood a word. Then he fell down and the cheers broke out again.

John remembered going down to the coast with Bob later to see him, Bob hoping to entice him to buy a plot, because other people would be certain to follow his example. And – Christ! – it must have been Juana who served dinner. Yes, a pretty girl with an olive-skinned face, it was coming back; provocative eyes and a way of walking that made Bob stare. My lord's mouth opened and closed several times before he got out: 'A sensation, my dear f-fellow. A complete tra-transformation – try my rum special – I take pr-pride in the change. An excellent horsewoman, na-native ability.'

Everyone's eyes had fixed on her generous body as she brought in the next course. Juana! John hardly heard what Cristobal was saying:

'And Miguel thought because she'd gone to El Mayorazgo after their quarrel it meant she loved him. He should have known better. He'd already bought her a bracelet which she refused. Three nights in a row before he killed himself he came up to the village to see her, but she never came out of her house. That's when he started to go mad.'

'No, hombre, no.' Pepe turned on him, and a group of men in the bar slowly turned to look. 'She wasn't at home, that's all it was.'

How had Miguel come to know her, John asked.

Juana was his wife's best friend, Pepe said. She was the only woman Pepe had ever known Miguel pluck up the courage to talk to. 'Now and again he'd see one he liked and he'd say, "I'll try her," but when the time came he always went home. "Another time perhaps ..."' And yet he was lively, always making jokes. But he didn't know how to talk, make compliments to a girl, though in other ways he was more of a man than any Pepe knew.

But once he got up the courage, she was the only woman for him. At first, he hadn't wanted her to go down to the coast, Pepe said. 'I told him it was better that she didn't go. But later he changed his mind, thinking she could earn well and save money working for a foreigner.'

'A girl who's broken with one betrothed can't be trusted,' said Cristobal, as though stating an eternal truth. Pepe ignored him.

What else had Miguel said?

Pepe sat silent for a time. Then he said: 'When I told him I was leaving Culito to see if I could get work on the dam, I encouraged him to come with me. But he said he wanted to wait. If he'd done what I said this wouldn't have happened, that's what I think. But with the money he'd got saved up, I thought, he could buy fodder, hold out for a few months.'

'He never said anything more to you about getting work on the dam?'

'No.'

'You're sure?'

'Yes.'

'Did he say anything else? Anything at all?'

Pepe shook his head. It was true, Miguel hadn't talked much towards the end, but Pepe thought he told him everything because they were friends.

When had he seen him last?

'Two nights before ... He was dispirited, yes, but I thought it was one of those things that would pass. It's true, I hadn't seen him like that before, he was usually so carefree. I never thought he could do anything like this.'

'Never saw any signs before?'

'Never. He was the last person I would have believed it of.'

'Then why did he do it?'

Pepe shook his head sadly. He didn't know. When Miguel came out of the señorita's house, he went down the street to Josefa's shop. Pepe heard this later from her. He stood in the doorway for a while, looking in. There were other customers and she didn't think much of it at the time, though later she remembered how white he looked. She wondered if he'd had a bit too much to drink. 'Then he went in and said he needed some rope. She saw he was sober, and put a coil on the counter. He stretched it between his arms and tested it. "Stronger than that," he said, smiling. She'll remember that smile all her life, she says. He found the rope he wanted and paid for it. "I wouldn't have sold it to him if I'd known why he wanted it. Never. Except for his pallor he looked the Miguel I'd always known, the young man who always knew his mind."'

22

18 September

I pulled out the last sheet of Pepe's words from the typewriter and went to the window. It was 3 a.m. and the street was dead to the world. For a few hours the village slept in a silence mocked by the brightness of the moon which hung like an African mask overhead.

On a new sheet of paper I jotted:

Five hours of talk and only a slender yield of first-hand evidence. Miguel's joviality in the past came as a surprise. But after the quarrel he felt 'lost'; those who've insisted on the importance of the break with Juana are right. Then there's his decision not to accompany Pepe to work on the dam. It's puzzling. What was there to wait for at El Mayorazgo? The wait must have proved fruitless because when he came, finally, to ask me for work on the dam, he had no other hope. Two nights before the end he was 'dispirited', it was the night after he saw I wasn't going to help. He said nothing of this to Pepe.

All the rest is circumstantial: the cause of the quarrel, his attempts to see Juana three nights running and his visit, on the third and last night, to María Burgos. Only someone very close to Miguel – Ana perhaps – could provide indisputable facts. Daunting as the thought is at the moment, I shall have to talk to her.

If one looks beyond 'facts', however, one could say that these talks have yielded some unexpected results. By comparison, as it were.

This, for example: compare Pepe with Miguel. Pepe demonstrated that it's possible for a sharecropper to stand up to his landlord and make him give way. Perhaps Pepe is exceptional; but Miguel had as much cause for complaint. He 'respected the señorita too much,' Pepe says.

Then contrast Miguel's inability to stand up to María Burgos with his decisiveness as her sharecropper: innovative, shrewd, prepared to take calculated risks. He must have made more money for her (as both must have known) than any other sharecropper. But it gave him no confidence to stand up to her, one has to conclude.

There's another comparison which Pepe himself made. Miguel was not like other village men in his relationship with women. He betrayed a lack of assertiveness towards individual women and, simultaneously, an assertion of male dominance over the *role* of women. He filled only half the male role as defined here.

And finally, the contrast with his older brother and his father, as described by Dolores. Antonio resolute, rebellious, militant. His father authoritarian, proud, stubbornly refusing change. Both, without doubt, 'men', the men who dominated Miguel's childhood, and difficult to live up to. Each, almost certainly, setting a different example to the boy. Miguel, one can imagine, may have felt he could never be the 'man' both his father and his brother expected him to be.

Whichever way one looks at it, these 'differentials' represent no real advance. Reduced to a series of comparisons with others, Miguel, the man with a hoe on a terrace of corn standing in the centre of his own world, vanishes. This fragmentary evidence will only make sense when restored to the way he made his own life.

23

Two days later John got up his courage and set off to walk down the familiar track to the coast. His talks with Dolores and Pepe had made him realize that the search for Miguel was going to be more difficult than he had anticipated; the idea of creating a 'memorial' to Miguel was plainly an illusion. At best, he saw now, the attempt to give meaning to Miguel's life was no more than an effort to make up for the meaning he had not accorded him in life. An unworthy return, an indulgence perhaps – a writer's (or lover's) impossible desire to be inside the other, to taste life from there. It was imperative now to talk to people who had entered his world with such desire.

Nonetheless, the prospect of the forthcoming encounter with Juana made John nervous. She would look at him, he imagined, with eyes narrowing, thinking he'd come to make trouble. A foreigner! 'No, I've nothing to say, I don't know anything,' and her face would close in peasant blankness over the wrought-iron gate and he'd be left looking at the clipped English lawn and weeping willow, at gardeners watering the hybrid teas Bughleigh was proud of having imported from England. And Juana would turn her back and walk away down the marble path into the house and the kitchen my lord likes to show off: Aga, refrigerator, oak table specially hauled from London – and the opportunity would be lost.

That was to be avoided. It would be better to ask for Bughleigh straight away – the pretext of Bob's plans would do – and ask his advice. All these people on the coast loved to talk about their deals. He'd heard them at Bob's fiesta at the dam down there still just out of sight. Each trying to outbid the other with the claim to have bought cheapest and, in a rabid auction of English common sense, relate the most outrageous story of Spanish inefficiency, ignorance and sloth.

'Of course, land up here in Benalamar is cheaper, but it's not liveable, what!'

'Only a question of time before it develops. Bob's going to urbanize all this land, don't you know? Lay out roads, gardens … Good value, I'd say. Plenty of water what with the dam.'

'But can they build, that's what I say. I had to show my workmen what a toilet roll holder was for.'

Amidst the guffaws, the wine flowed from the carafes the muleteers silently unloaded before joining the workmen in their patched and bleached cottons at the other end of the trestle tables. Two distinct worlds. And then a Knightsbridge voice:

'You'll be laying out a golf course, won't you, Bob? Look at this land, it'd make a perfect eighteen holes …'

Bob smiled defensively at the jibe. Under the table the not-so-Knightsbridge wife rubbed her leg against John's.

'What a wonderful country this is! I know, it's not really modern but that's what makes it so charming.'

A stupefied Bughleigh rose onto his chair and, amid cheers, started to declaim. The ruined blonde's hand wandered to John's thigh. 'Why don't we ever see you down on the coast?' she whispered drunkenly.

At the other end, the workmen had got a boy from one of the farms drunk and he was sprawled on his face.

'I've always wanted to make love in that ruined castle outside Torre del Mar. Fifteenth century!' Her hand fumbled with his fly. At that moment, along the rim of the gorge, John saw Ana passing; she didn't look down but she couldn't help but hear the revelling below. He got up suddenly, the wine swirling in his head, thinking to call out to her; just then Bughleigh collapsed amidst cheers and he sat down again.

'My God, he bores you so with his poetry,' the woman said in John's ear. 'Nothing he likes better than being wanked off while he's reading – who is it? Ah, Dante, that's right.'

John imagined she had the information first hand in every sense, and thought it wisest to escape before, *manu militari*, she ambushed him …

This arid earth a golf course! The morning air, as he walked down the track now, was as clear as a lens, the silence mineral sharp. Everything was visible and yet somehow invisible, and he realized with a shock that there was no one about on the terraces, which stood out in sharp relief. No activity, no men working, hoeing, breaking the earth to give a visible meaning to the terraces which, in silence and dust, seemed to be reverting soundlessly, endlessly to nature again. A couple of tethered goats came towards him anxiously, hopefully, as though no human had passed this way. Below, the white dots of farmsteads, close by yet separate, each just large enough in ordinary times for a family to subsist on half of what was produced; now no sound came from them.

To his surprise he saw a line of men emerging from the watercourse, raising dust on the track. Gauging his footholds rock to rock, John hurried down to meet them, knowing they must be from the dam. In front walked the foreman, old Salvador, with his hooked nose set in a deeply wrinkled face.

'Hola, Salvador! What's happening?'

The foreman lifted his sombrero and wiped his forehead. The other men piled up behind him and spread out.

'Well?'

'They came and stopped the work. They say charges have been laid against the dam.'

'What? Who came?'

'The Guardia Civil.' His voice was expressionless; the others stood staring beneath the straw rims of their hats.

'Miguel Alarcón's mother?' John asked.

'No, the mayor's order they said.'

Bewildered, John sat on a rock and wiped his face. Then he asked the foreman what he was going to do.

'Go and inform Sr Bob, that's all we can do.'

'Yes, good. He'll know what to do.' But what was there to do? Things had gone further than he'd imagined. He watched the men going off; the last to move was José, with whom John had once sheltered, laughing together, as a shower of stones hurtled over them when they were dynamiting rock for the dam. He came from the farm below El Mayorazgo.

'José,' John called. There seemed no point now in going down to Bughleigh's. 'Have you got a minute?'

'Sí, señor.'

They moved into the shade of a carob where the air changed not only in temperature but in quality, becoming like water. John gave him a cigarette which he lit, scratching the wheel on the flint of a cord lighter.

'Do you mind if I ask you a few things? You knew Miguel, didn't you?'

For nearly two hours they sat under the tree talking. At last, John thought, as he climbed up the track, the small spark might have lit.

24

20 September

José and Miguel were childhood friends. One of José's earliest memories was not of their games but – his voice dropped to a whisper – the day the church was fired! Miguel's mother must have brought him up to the village and left him in José's house because the two of them ran out together to watch. They were only small, five or six. There were people rushing everywhere, some piling religious objects in the square to set fire to them, others secretly trying to save whatever they could find. Men armed with shotguns were shouting, women crying. It was frightening, a bad thing to see …

And then suddenly Antonio, Miguel's brother, appeared; the two boys hid, and they heard him shouting at the men: 'What are you doing? Is this the revolution we've been waiting for so long? The revolution isn't made with stupidities like this.' But some of the men pointed their guns at him and told him to shut up. Even he couldn't stop them.

The two boys had run home frightened, not daring to say what they'd seen … José paused and rolled a cigarette which he offered to me. Then he said:

'One other time, I remember, we were together in the square. A village assembly, something to do with the revolution.'

Antonio got up on the fountain and spoke – about the land, was it? – and lots of labourers cheered. The land for those who worked it. When he jumped down he saw Miguel in the crowd and lifted him onto his shoulder, almost covering him in a red and black neckerchief. Miguel was so proud he repeated the moment endlessly to José. But his father was angry when he heard of it, Miguel told him.

Antonio always treated Miguel affectionately. José remembered him taking the boy by the hand and walking together, showing him insects and small animals. He was always talking, telling Miguel things. He got angry if Miguel broke off a fly's wing. 'But when the revolution, as they called it, ended and our forces came, Antonio vanished.'

The year before Miguel's father got El Mayorazgo, José's father had a stroke of luck and was able to rent a farmstead from a colonel who never visited the land he'd won at cards. Rearing a calf each year paid the rent, so José's family was better off than Miguel's. Even so, the farmstead couldn't support José's three older brothers who had to go out day-labouring whenever they could find work until they were called up by the Franquista army. The civil war was still being fought elsewhere; in Benalamar it was over.

The two boys were virtual neighbours again. Their fathers sent the seven-year-olds out to tend small flocks of goats which they often pastured together. But sometimes Miguel vanished for days looking for fresh pastures. His goats, José recalled, were always the best fed and biggest … 'I expect he'd learnt a few tricks from his father who'd been a goatherd. We only quarrelled once, when I caught him breaking off branches of a carob on my grandfather's land, the land Sr Bob bought, to feed his goats, but in a few days we were friends again.'

The day the war ended for Benalamar there was uproar in the village; the church bell pealed all day long, victorious shouts and the sound of martial music swept in gusts over the countryside. The revolutionary militiamen had fled in disarray, and the sharecroppers and small-holders flocked to join in the celebrations. A lorry-load of soldiers and falangists churned up the dirt road to take the village where the local falangists had come out of hiding and were already in command. That night, José started awake at the sound of half a dozen rifle volleys. He feared the war had started again; the next morning his father told him not to be stupid.

'Did you hear them?' he asked Miguel as they joined their flocks. Miguel nodded. 'What were they shooting, rabbits?'

Miguel called his goats. 'Come on, there's pasture by the boulder.'

José didn't understand. He wanted to play hopscotch in the dust with Miguel or kick the bag filled with old bits of cloth which served as a football. But Miguel was already walking on.

They both went barefoot, their shirts and trousers cut down from older brothers', worn and patched. Miguel wore a battered sombrero that came down over his ears – which José envied and often tried to snatch from his head because he never took it off. But now he just followed him.

By the boulder Miguel stopped and pointed.

José saw blood staining the rock. 'What is it?' he whispered. 'Blood.'

'But of what animal's?'

Neither could take his eyes off the red stains.

'Look there,' said Miguel pointing at the freshly turned earth. 'That's where the falangists buried them.'

'Come on, let's go.' Trembling, José grabbed the goats' tether and pulled them away. He remembers his fear to this day. 'Miguel!' he shouted. 'Vamos!'

But when José looked back he saw Miguel standing there

with his eyes under the sombrero fixed on the rock; that day he didn't see him again.

'Could he have thought his brother Antonio was one of those who'd been shot?'

'No. Because one day I asked him where Antonio was. And he said, "I'm not telling ..."

"That's because you don't know, burro!"

"I know. Antonio told me where he was going. He told me what he had to do. The night before he left he explained it to me. So, stupid!"'

José made a grab for his hat. 'If you know so much, tell me why he ran away.'

'He didn't. My brother's not a coward like those who run off and hide.' Miguel punched José on the arm: 'He's gone to fight.'

'A las barricadas, a las barricadas ...' José chanted defiantly at him. 'He's a Red. And when he comes back ...'

The next thing José knew he was flat on his back with Miguel standing over him. 'He isn't,' he cried, 'he's never coming back.' And José saw the tears of rage in his eyes.

After that José didn't remember him talking about Antonio. 'And I didn't ask, either. My father said we should forget what had happened, it was better not to talk about it. No one talked about it. Everything was peaceful, just as it had always been, the trouble-makers were gone.' José had come to forget Miguel had a brother until the war ended and people from the Red side started to come back. A lot of them were court-martialled, some were shot and many went to prison, José remembered. But Antonio never came back and José never asked what had happened.

'It was perhaps just as well he didn't return,' I said.

'Well, he never got on with his father, that's for sure,' José replied, mistaking my meaning. One day he'd brought his goats up the track to wait for Miguel and he'd seen the two men standing under the vine. The old man was shouting at Antonio and raised his arm as though to strike him. Antonio went on talking quietly, José could hear what he said. It was the time of the revolution and the collective; Antonio was telling him he should join.

As José watched the two men, Miguel came round from the back with the goats and stood looking at his brother and father. Then his father shouted at him to get the goats out to pasture, and he rounded them up and joined José without a word.

'What's wrong with your father?' José asked when they were out of earshot.

'Nothing. Antonio should show more respect.'

'You mean, he sided with his father!' I exclaimed.

'Miguel always respected his father, it's natural, isn't it? A son doesn't quarrel with what his father says.'

'Was he like his father?'

'No, he was smaller, his father was a tall man. Once, they say, he carried a dead man on his back five leagues over the mountains without stopping. Another goatherd who was killed by a landslide.'

'In character, I meant.'

'Character? Well, Miguel laughed a lot and I never saw his father even smile. Miguel was a good neighbour, you know; he always had time to lend a hand if you asked; he'd come and see if there was anything you needed. His father wasn't like that, he kept to himself. He'd been a goatherd and was used to being on his own, I suppose, it's a different life. Gone for three months up to the high pastures in summer, back again in the autumn, always moving. He didn't have to depend on neighbours as we do at times.'

By the time the war ended in 1939, both Miguel and José were nine and old enough to be earning. They became look-outs for the señorita's olive mill, which was shipping out black-market oil. The boys took it in turns to sit in a cave by the church to watch for a car; if one came it could only be an inspector's, and they ran to the mill to give warning. Then, on top of the aftermath of war came drought and the hunger years. José was lucky to get a job with a miner digging a well half a day's walk away; stuck in water all day, earning twelve pesetas, ten for his father and two for himself. Miguel was sent by his father to the sierra to herd his uncle's goats, and José didn't see him for a year and a half.

'There were outlaws in the sierra then, weren't there?'

'Yes, and there still were until a few years ago.' José came across them sometimes when he smuggled tobacco over the mountains to the villages beyond. They'd call out from their hiding place for him to stop, and to be on the safe side he'd give them some tobacco. There were a good two dozen of them, mainly Reds, he thought, who'd fled to the mountains when the Franquista forces took this part of Spain, and they were armed with rifles and pistols. They had spies everywhere and anyone who informed on them was in certain danger. Once in a while, until he knew he'd been killed in the war, José wondered if Antonio were among them.

By now things were so bad in the village that some people died of the complications of malnutrition. Then came salvation of a kind: the sierra was to be planted with pines. Miguel, who'd returned after his uncle was killed by the outlaws, José and most of the villagers were soon working on the slopes closest to Benalamar.

This was when José saw Miguel change. The boy who, like his father, rarely smiled, was now a cheerful, lively and determined youth. It was Miguel who said they should be ashamed to sign for their wages with thumbprints, and organized lessons in the evening from the lame schoolmaster.

'Come on,' he said to José, 'you don't want to end up an illiterate sharecropper. It's time to learn something now.' After a time José joined him, but Miguel was already so far advanced that he knew he could never catch up. Miguel learnt to read and write and do sums so fast it seemed to José he had them already in his head. When he got an idea he wouldn't let it go. But he'd always laugh and joke about it, too.

José's gentle eyes lit up at the memory of Miguel's carefree success. This was a Miguel I had never seen.

'Well, with a foreigner he'd be more formal perhaps, but with his friends he was always laughing and joking,' José replied. Until the last days when he changed, and became more like the boy he'd been: withdrawn and unsmiling. José thought it was because of Juana, his *novia*. He knew they'd quarrelled, but didn't think much about it. Miguel rarely spoke about it to him.

'Why was that, do you think?'

'Perhaps he was ashamed …'

'Have you got a *novia*, José? Yes? What would you do if she left you?'

'Left me!' His head jerked up. 'My *novia* – no, she wouldn't so much as talk to another man … Miguel shouldn't have trusted Juana, she'd been betrothed once before.'

'You wouldn't trust a man who'd had more than one *novia*?'

'Ah, that's not the same, is it? A man and a woman are different.' He rubbed his cigarette out on a rock, taking care to see no embers remained.

I repressed a flash of anger. 'What I meant, José, is what does a man feel if it happens?'

'Ah, to get himself or her out of the way. There was one here, two or three years ago it must have been, who waited for his former betrothed by the spring and stabbed her to death. And then he hanged himself.'

'But not everyone is capable of killing, are they?'

'No ... But then a man suffers inside, his self-respect is gone, he doesn't want to be seen. That's how it was with Miguel, his pride must have suffered, any man's would, especially after taking her on when she'd been betrothed before. Even all the money he'd put by didn't help in the end because it was his self-respect that had gone.'

'What was he saving for, do you think? Did he ever say?'

'No, never ... Ay yes! Not so long ago, he said he was going to buy a gold bracelet. If Juana didn't want it, he'd give it to another female. It must have been after she broke off with him. But if he bought it he didn't give it to anyone else that I know of.'

'If you had a lot of money saved, what would you do, José?'

'Me? Well, I'll never have it, so it's not worth thinking about. Until the dam, I only had casual work, going round at night looking for a job for the next day and as often as not the work had already been given. There are so many looking for work that if ever a farm comes up to sharecrop there's a rush.'

'There's no other future?'

'You can't think of a future, there's only today and how to get through it. Once, when I was doing my military service in the north, I thought of crossing over to France. But not long before they caught someone who tried. And when a man's away, the pueblo is what he yearns for, yet here ...'

Had Miguel done military service at the same time? No, José said, he was excused as the only son. But there was something about him wanting to join the army once and his father wouldn't sign the papers. So Miguel had stayed; it was just as well, José said, because not long after, his father died of a heart attack in the fields and Miguel took over El Mayorazgo.

An inescapable emptiness opened before me. Everything seemed cut off, frontiers, future, new possibilities. People stayed on, clung to the soil as the only handhold in life, fearful of spinning off the face of the earth.

'So people stay … If a farm came your way would you be willing to sharecrop?'

'Of course. If there was a farm free … With a bit of land you can grow enough for yourself most years to get by. That's the main thing, what else is there?'

'And if you owned your own farm you'd get by that much better. I've been wondering whether that was what Miguel was trying to achieve.'

'To have land for yourself is what everyone wants, you're independent then. But here most of the land is in the hands of a few. In any case, he never spoke of things like that … No, poor guy, nothing turned out right for him in the end. Everything came at once, the drought, the *novia* and the señorita breaking off the deal. I suppose something got in his head …'

25

On an impulse, that afternoon John went to see Tío Bigote. The old man was sitting plaiting esparto by the door of the red cottage and paid no attention to his approach. Coming down the hill in front of the house, John saw, to his surprise, a few rows of young maize growing close to the borehole on a terrace that elsewhere had turned to dust. From the borehole a thin trickle of water meandered, accumulated in a small pool and was swallowed up by the earth.

John stopped a few paces in front of the old man and only then did he look up. The extravagant moustache flaring out under the craggy nose, the deep-set eyes beneath the sombrero, reminded him of pictures of nineteenth-century Andalusian bandits. He was not a man one approached with ease. John commented on his fortune in still having water.

'Three years' hard tunnelling, if that's fortune,' he replied curtly.

Well, John said, it was fortune today; the work had paid off.

'A man with foresight's worth two without.' Tío Bigote went on plaiting. John looked around; in the shed at the side of the house he saw two calves tied up. He'd managed well: was one Miguel's?

No, those were his. 'And why do you ask?'

'Because Miguel sold you his …'

'And I returned it as everyone knows.'

'Why?'

He raised his head slowly and stared at John; his eyes were as hard as bullets. 'A man's deals are his own business.'

Of course, John replied. He didn't mean to intrude, but he was interested in Miguel. Had he said why he was breaking the deal?

'A man doesn't go back on his word.'

'That's what I mean.'

The old man was silent. Then: 'And what is your interest in Miguel?'

'He was a friend.'

'You are asking many questions, it's said.'

Maybe. John shrugged.

'I gave the calf back to his sister. Miguel didn't ask. And that's all I have to say.'

Dismissed, John walked back up the track until he found a eucalyptus out of sight of the red cottage and sat in its shade. The conversation, concluded so abruptly, had rattled him. Was the old man hiding something? It seemed like it. But what was there to hide? Wasn't the implication rather that he'd been willing to listen to Ana where he would have refused Miguel? To a woman, who hadn't given – perhaps couldn't give – her word rather than to a man who had given his? Probably. In any case, Tío Bigote had a reputation as a difficult, taciturn man. All the same, John realized, he'd missed a chance: he hadn't asked how he came to be one of the few who owned a farm, how he had overcome the obstacle that others faced. He was on the point of returning when he thought better of it; he might catch Tío Bigote in a more communicative mood another day.

In any case, his relative prosperity was evident. A trickle of water to grow maize for two calves. Money enough presumably to buy extra fodder. Independence. The one-eyed in the kingdom of the blind.

John stretched out on the warm earth, as he used to do with a book, looking up at the sunlight tingeing the transparent leaves. Perhaps, he thought, the old man's tight-lipped brusqueness was like Miguel's father's. One could imagine him also never taking his hat off indoors or out. The same sort of pride in his self-sufficiency; a personal autarky demanding constant assertion; curt commands to his sons in order to stave off challenges to his authority. Beneath it all, fear that the edifice could collapse.

John tried to imagine Miguel's childhood ... One could take the memories of others, he reflected, and turn them inside out, see them from Miguel the child's point of view. But memories weren't 'the thing once known'. They were the thing as it's remembered as having been known, almost inevitably re-elaborated over the years ... And could one be sure that Miguel had lived those events in the way others remembered them?

There was another option: take these memories as scattered indications and trace the lines between them. Like one of those puzzles in which points have to be linked to reveal the image waiting to be disclosed. But here there were no numbers indicating the points. To draw across the gaps required a leap of the imagination; a leap with both feet on the ground.

He began the long climb back. Themes, not lines; existential links between the things already known ... And then suddenly he wondered what the hell he was doing, turning Miguel's life into a puzzle of lines. Where had this abstraction come from? Was it connected to the fascination he felt in collecting stories about Miguel? The feeling that he was living through and for these stories, denying his own existence except as a recipient of others' stories? Living vicariously, but more intensely than when his nose was plunged in a book, the collector now of others' lives? Ah yes, all this was comforting because it allowed him to deny his own problems, his guilt, in the name of a superior objective, the search for Miguel. His original guilty obsession had covered its tracks, he saw, and reappeared under the guise of the intellectual determined to solve a puzzle – Miguel's death.

The dust was hot underfoot and his shirt clung to his back. Guilt was, and remained, the reason for this passion to bring Miguel back to life in some way, he thought. And he'd best recognize it lest blindness led him to fall into other traps.

These thoughts, not surprisingly, brought him up against a blank wall. Recognizing repressed motivations told him nothing about how he might proceed. Would it be better to try simply to *feel* Miguel's childhood – imagine it? Let his mind flow round it until he found a path to pursue? But wasn't there something equally abstract in thinking that such a random process would lead anywhere?

Perplexed, he found the shade of an olive. Until he had the nub of an insight his imagination would fail him, that much he knew. It was no good pretending there was a bone to chew, he had to have one. Something tangible, real, a structure of some sort. He began the climb up the path again.

Forgetting the heat and dust, thoughts started to flow through his head as sometimes they did when he was walking. Speculative reality fused with imagination as he thought of Miguel's childhood … Third of four children, Miguel before the war was certainly too young to have helped his father in the fields like Antonio. But also probably too old to receive baby Ana's attention and too healthy to need fussing over like his sick sister. Perhaps then he'd found no distinct place of his own, especially in his father's distant eyes.

If anyone gave him a place it would be Antonio, who instructed and confided in him, suggested that life held other possibilities from those their father unquestioningly accepted. But it would have been a contentious place. Antonio's beliefs challenged the father, threatened family disruption. The civil war would have drawn a front line between the two men. At stake was a future being fought over on battlefields beyond the mountains; there were no neutrals now.

John fell into a rhythmic walk that carried his feet effortlessly upwards, unaware of anything now but a mythic past unravelling in his head.

These two men, self-willed, each tacitly demanding the boy's allegiance. Loyalty to one is betrayal of the other, a betrayal of filial/fraternal love. The boy is split. Faced with choosing one or the other – an impossible choice – he will take sides, now with his father ('Antonio should show more respect'), now with his brother when they're out of earshot; but nothing heals the sense that he's unworthy of, insufficient to, either.

The brief revolution is defeated, shot down and buried. Antonio is forced to escape; he has led Miguel so far and then abandons him, and the boy reacts with rage. By the age of seven he has lost a brother and sister. His father is right: hiding the señorita in his cowshed, he staked his life on a future where nothing would change. The world is a quantum from which his job is to wrest a daily subsistence: self-sufficiency, the small world where his word is still law. He has not changed.

Even before Antonio flees, Miguel is out minding goats. His father needs him. Scouring the countryside for pasture where other children want to play, he is determined to make a success of the task. He has a place now – a value – in his father's eyes. By the time he's nine, he's earning his first day-wage for the family as the señorita's look-out. Despite the difficult times, he perhaps feels more secure than in the past: each evening he hands over his wage to his mother with a certain pride. But drought and the post-war chaos bring wide-spread hunger; money buys nothing any longer. Without warning, his father orders his exile to the mountains. There he loses everything that is familiar: family, farmstead and village. An eleven-year-old in the sierra's wilderness, he possibly even loses a sense of himself. It takes another loss – his uncle's death at the hands of the outlaws – to bring him back to El Mayorazgo.

John found himself in the street leading to his house. These thoughts, he knew, would lose their intimate congruence as soon as he put them on paper, lie uncertainly there waiting to be given a content that was no longer inherent in them. Signposts, which as in his childhood during the war, had been pointed in arbitrary directions to confuse the invader. And there were still so few of them. Next to nothing was known about Miguel's mother, for example, other than that she was a warm and loving woman whom Antonio loved and admired. Maybe both sons shared a closeness with her that made good the distance between them and their father. But her love was powerless before the patriarchal authoritarianism that ruled her sons.

Tomorrow, he told himself as he climbed the stairs wearily, he'd have to go down to the coast to see Juana. And every day it became more necessary to talk to Ana. He opened the granary door – what a relief it would be to be able to write without ever having to put a word on the page! – and saw, propped against the typewriter, a note in Bob's scratchy handwriting asking him to come by as soon as possible.

26

He was surprisingly calm for a change. He'd been to the town and hired good lawyers who had assured him that the case would go his way. Expert witnesses would prove that the dam was no threat to the safety of the farms, he'd draw up plans – there was no problem at all.

'Wait a minute,' John said. 'What's been happening?'

Bob explained. The mayor had used the pretext of Miguel's mother's charges to order work stopped. Bob's lawyers maintained he had no right to do so. It was an obvious ploy to pressure Bob into providing water for the village. The case brought by Miguel's mother would have to be heard but it would be confined to her charges about the dam, not water for the village. She wouldn't win because once he'd drawn plans it would be clear her allegations were groundless. As for expropriation, the mayor would first have to prove that there were no alternative sources of village water. 'He can't do that while he's digging his own well and has done nothing about deepening the old village borehole, can he?' Bob smiled, looking satisfied with himself.

'But what about water for the village? That's the real priority.'

'Yes,' said Bob. But he'd worked out that to get water from his borehole would cost the village more in pumping, piping and building a reservoir than to deepen the old one in the village square. 'That's why that expropriation business was just a con.'

'I see.' John had no way of judging Bob's claim. But something else had surprised him. Had Bob been building the dam without plans?

'Of course. It's the sort of thing you can do in your head. But they'll want to see some drawings. I'd be glad if you'd attend the case, your Spanish is better than mine and it'd be good if there were two of us – a combined front, you know.'

'I see.' Bob's involvement of him had come to irritate John. 'I don't know about the combined front,' he replied.

'Well, it's us against them when the chips are down.'

'I thought it was supposed to be us with them.'

'Yes, but if they don't want it that way …'

'They? It's been María Burgos, the mayor and now Miguel's mother. They're the only people who've caused trouble.'

'Well, María Burgos is on our side now,' Bob answered with a laugh.

'I don't see how she can be on our side if we're on the others'.'

Bob heard the edge in John's voice and replied equally sharply: 'Who're you talking about?'

'Her sharecroppers, for one.'

'Oh, for Christ's sake. They're going to benefit as much from the dam as she will.'

'Once they've paid you for the water, that's part of your deal with María Burgos, isn't it?'

'What d'you want me to do – give it to them?' Bob stared at him. Both were angry now.

'Yes, why not?'

'D'you know how much they stand to make by having all that water from the dam? A fortune! They can irrigate terraces they've never irrigated, grow two or three crops a year, plant new things.'

'And make María Burgos a fortune.' John remembered Miguel's bitterness at seeing Bob's land untilled; he didn't know the first thing about farming, wasn't interested. 'Actually,' John added provocatively, 'you could make the dam over to them and just keep the water you need.'

'What's got into you? You know bloody well they wouldn't maintain it; in a year or two it'd be useless, silted up, neglected.'

'I thought you'd say that. It's what Eden said about the Suez Canal, remember? A backward lot like the Egyptians couldn't run such a thing, soon there wouldn't be a ship able to use it. But they seem to have managed to keep it open, haven't they?'

'With the help of a lot of foreign technicians, I'll bet. But I'm not here to talk about that, I'm concerned about the water and the dam. I don't understand your attitude either. When you first came, you were shocked at the poverty. I remember your face when you saw the men bringing in brushwood. I thought you wanted to help do something about it, that's why I've involved you all along in the dam.'

'Uh! I no longer think you can benefit everyone in a set-up that's designed to benefit some more than others.'

'I never said everyone was going to benefit,' Bob replied. 'I said we could begin to change things here. And that's what I still believe.'

'Maybe. But I'm not interested in helping María Burgos. Kindness, good intentions – aid, if you like – are tied to particular interests, that's what I've come to see.'

Christ! Bob thought. How typical of these middle-class Oxbridge hair-splitters: they can't wipe their own arses! But he needed John and so all he said was: 'Of course, there are particular interests. That's what runs the world. You're not so utopian as to think that isn't the case, are you?'

'Let's be concrete, Bob. You had to compromise with María Burgos because she's the largest landowner here. How do you know there aren't going to be other compromises if you develop your land?'

'Well, I'll be concrete, to use your expression. Does the land provide work for everyone? No. Does the village? No. There are only two ways of trying to change that, as I see it. Make the land more fertile with irrigation and provide work by building. And who's going to build if it isn't the foreigners? It's starting already on the coast and it's going to get big.' His eyes shone with an intensity John recognized as conviction, if not necessarily honesty. 'Would you rather see the dam unfinished, people out of work, hungry?'

'You're putting words in my mouth. The point I'm making is about ownership, property.'

'That's the logic of what you're saying,' Bob interrupted. 'Leave things as they are. Live here like a tourist, pity these poor sods and when you go home entertain your dinner guests with stories of their poverty. Well, I'm not like that. I've learnt that if you want to get something done you've got to do it yourself.'

'On others' behalf?' John paused. Others, he was about to say, had tried to change things for themselves twenty years ago – but he could already hear Bob laughing: and look what happened to them! Instead he said: 'I don't believe tourism is a basis of development. It'll provide work for a couple of years and that's it.'

'What do you want: General Motors to set up an assembly plant?' Bob retorted. 'That would be development?'

'No. I don't know the answer, except that I don't think it lies just with you or me.'

'Well, it doesn't seem to lie with them, does it? They couldn't even get water out of the ground.' He fell silent, his eyes vacating the conversation: he might have foreseen, he thought, that John would become a windbag. They all did. No wonder England was in a mess. There were plenty, too many, like John in the Labour Party talking socialism and doing sweet FA about it. Get your hands dirty, mate, he wanted to say to them …

He looked at John: it was now or never.

'OK,' he said acquiescently, 'I'm in further than I bargained for, I've got my hands dirty. Bound to when you try to get something done – agreed? I'm not complaining, I honestly believe what I'm doing will bring improvements. You can disagree, but I can't think you'd really rather see the dam left unfinished.'

'Who's talking about leaving it unfinished?'

'I am.' He was almost out of money, he explained, and now, on top of everything else, he had to pay the lawyers. Bughleigh wouldn't make a down payment until he saw the dam filled. 'This is why I wanted to talk to you. Buy another plot, a couple if you can, and next year with water you'll be able to sell them at double the price. I guarantee you that.'

'I'm not a gambler, Bob.'

'There's no gamble in it. Or rather only one. Do you want to bring some sort of prosperity to Benalamar or not? Are you going to go back on everything you said and I thought you believed? Worse still, destroy one of the few hopes there is? That's the gamble.'

'You've loaded the question all right, but that's not the point. I haven't got any spare cash, it's as simple as that.'

Bob knew he was lying, it was written all over his face.

'All right,' he shrugged, lifting himself out of the chair. 'It's a pity after all this to be left facing both ways, eh? The case is Friday week at five. Are you coming?'

'If you want.'

'I'll see you there, if not before.'

On his way home, John reflected on the curiosity of Bob's use of the words 'dirty hands'. Surely he'd never heard of Sartre's play, Bob didn't read … This petty vengeance failed to tranquillize his conscience, however. Was he right to jeopardize the dam? Was that what Miguel would have wanted? Were hastily defined principles more important than water?

Unsure of himself, he went to the granary to fetch a book. He remembered underlining the sentence where among Baudelaire's many torments, Sartre locates the poet's real affliction: indifference – the basic impossibility of taking himself or his acts as mattering seriously … An inner vacuum that, as he listened to himself arguing with Bob, had again been revealed. It was more important to him to fill this vacuum with speculations about Miguel and the past than to do something concrete about the future. Indifference was the easy way out, always had been. For what, in the last resort, did motives matter – even Bob's suspect motives – if they created conditions that would make Miguel's plight impossible in the future? Tomorrow, he decided, he'd write Bob a note; but first he'd go down to the coast.

27

21 September

Juana came to the gate, as impassive as I'd expected: the señor had gone out but would be coming back soon, so I said I would wait. After a time I followed her into the kitchen and asked for a drink of water. She fetched a glass and, with a certain nonchalance, opened a drink cupboard and indicated the bottles. I shook my head. 'Just water?' Her eyes were mocking.

'Even if it isn't as good as Benalamar water.'

'There's none to compare with it,' she said and we began to talk fitfully about the village. I was almost sure she wouldn't have heard the news of the mayor's and priest's dismissals last night, though in the village no one had been talking of anything else. Everyone had a different story, but there was common agreement that Miguel's mother had had something to do with it: the scandal of Miguel's burial was too great to cover up, it appears. I kept the news to myself to use at an opportune moment.

Evasive – no, laconic, sharp – Juana stood by the Aga, and I felt her consciousness of the desire she aroused and held away, tantalizingly. I envied Miguel, pitied him. Her beauty, her luxuriant body, seemed to demand attention, her own as much as others', quite unlike Ana's unawareness. She fenced, parrying with irony; but when at last I told her, her guard fell.

'Madre mia! Dismissed? Because of …?'

'Yes, it was enough.'

'It was enough what they did,' she murmured, seeming not to know which way to turn. And then she blurted: 'I couldn't know he would do such a thing. He knew it was over, I gave the bracelet back.'

'You never suspected?'

'No, never. Those last nights when he came to my house in the village I didn't show myself. What more could I do?'

'Given him hope, perhaps.'

'Hope? For nothing? No. He shouldn't have insisted, he was – ah! One shouldn't speak of the dead in this way … I can't forgive, he killed something, wanting everything his way.' Her hand went to her forehead, smoothed her hair. The agitation didn't show yet, was constrained by the gesture.

'What was it?'

'Everything. He couldn't see that I've got a life. He was stupid, like all of them. What he wanted was one of those women who stays at home sewing all day, submissives who say yes to your face and no behind your back. I'm not like that.'

The words cut her off like a door slamming. We stood for a time. 'You didn't love him?' I said at last.

'No.' Suddenly she was no longer a mask. Her voice fell: her mother had pressed her to marry Miguel, who was a good match, a sharecropper with money, and because she respected her mother … 'I tried but I couldn't. My eyes have been opened.'

'Opened?'

'Yes,' and she looked round the large kitchen, 'opened. The foreigners are showing us that things can be different, they treat us like humans, even if we are poor and have to work. The señoritos have no respect for us. Fifty pesetas a month and what's left on the plate …'

I shook my head, thinking of Dolores and the superficiality

of the comment. She meant she wouldn't exchange this house for Miguel's farmstead.

She didn't deny it. 'Until the foreigners came there was nothing, no hope. But now there's work, more money, new things. In the village the people point at me, I know. Miguel worried about the things the neighbours said. But why should I? I told him, they've got nothing else to do, what is there in the pueblo? We should go to the town. But he wouldn't.'

'And that's when you broke with him?'

Yes, she said, but there'd been trouble before: his ordering her not to ride, not to cut her hair, not to wear trousers. 'Madre mia! There was no freedom.'

'He was jealous, perhaps.' She flashed a glance to see what I meant and understood.

'People think the worst,' she answered tartly. 'If an employer treats you like a human being they start to gossip. That's how it is here.'

'Was he worse than the others?'

'No, not at the beginning, he was more gentle, timid ...' She reflected. 'If he had remained – ah, why do I say this? He seemed nervous with women, I don't know why, the other men used to laugh at him and the girls kept away. He didn't know how to talk ... So they said straight away I was after his money. Stupid ... After a time he began to change, I don't know whether it was because of his friends or his mother. It was as though once he was sure of me he wanted me to do everything he said. They probably told him that a *novia* must watch what the people say. That was the trouble, he wasn't strong enough. The others think they're born to it, but with him it was different, he thought he couldn't be a man if he didn't do what the others do.'

She spoke very rapidly, almost in a whisper. Our voices were murmurs covered by the swishing of the sprinkler watering the lawn.

'He didn't want to leave?'

She shook her head, she had tried to persuade him but he wouldn't hear of it. He had his family to support. 'And with that María Burgos who prays in church she'll live for ever to go on robbing.' Miguel became annoyed when she spoke the truth, and told her not to say it again. 'And what are you going to do with the money the señorita doesn't take?' – and he had said, 'With money you can buy what you want.' She had said, 'Remember the hunger years, there was money but nothing to buy,' and he'd answered, 'With land and a pair of arms you can live.' – 'In the same way as now?' 'Better,' he'd smiled.

'What did it mean?'

'He thought one day he'd have enough money to buy a farm. That's what he said once.' Juana gave an impression of unconcern; he had refused her what she wanted, there was no more to be said. Then, unexpectedly, she added: 'He wasn't one for spending money, it cost him an effort. Saving was easy, but not spending, he was strange that way. He had a lot of money. The bracelet must have a cost a lot but …' She shrugged.

'You don't regret anything?' The dispassion, the distance she took in talking about him was disconcerting; her agitation came only when she felt herself implicated.

'Regret? Yes, how can I not regret? But I don't blame myself. I never lied, he knew what I thought. I didn't wish him any harm, the harm he did was to himself.'

'You might have prevented it. The people say –' I caught myself and stopped. 'I mean, why did you go to El Mayorazgo after you'd broken with him, it isn't the custom, is it?'

'Let the people say what they want, they've been talking about me since I was little because of my father. But if you want to know it was my mother's doing. She was thirsty from the walk up, and she took the opportunity of stopping at the farm.

She wanted me to patch things up with Miguel and that was her way of trying. It was a mistake and I regret it.'

She turned to look out of the window but there was no one there.

'It gave him hope ...'

'I didn't see him again. He was stubborn, once he had an idea he wouldn't let go.'

'He loved you, didn't he?'

'That was his way. He had an idea ... It was a mistake from the start. I'm sorry it happened, but especially I pity his mother and sister. The family has had no luck. Miguel needed a country girl, someone like his sister, born to the country.'

'But ...' The distinction seemed untenable; surely everyone in Benalamar was more or less born to the country.

'Ah no, the village isn't the countryside,' she said in a tone that made me smile. 'Some of the people who live in the country don't come up to the village more than once a month. Not much happens in the village, but there's even less in the country. That's why I wanted to go to the town. If Miguel had agreed, perhaps then today ...' For the first time a slender chance appeared in her eyes, a hope that as rapidly vanished. 'No,' she said, picking up a saucepan, 'it couldn't have been. He would never leave.'

'And you wouldn't stay?'

'No. Not in the way he wanted me to.'

'The land meant that much to him?'

'The land or his idea.'

'What was it?'

'I don't know, it was there but he couldn't say it. I think his mother and sister were part of it, they didn't like my being his *novia*, they made me feel it.'

Was this another self-justification? A way of excusing her part? Impossible to tell. The bland manner, the new reasons,

reasons whose logic remained opaque at each turn, made me suspicious. 'Why?' I asked.

'How can one know? Perhaps they were frightened he would leave.'

'They knew you wanted to?'

'Yes. But they knew he wouldn't, he wouldn't leave them. His mother, especially, she was always telling him things. Warning him about me, saying I'd come between them.'

'Were they that close?'

'As close as two fingers. Miguel wouldn't do anything without asking her, he let her treat him like a child. That was another thing that got on my nerves. He was always going to be hers more than mine.'

'He was the only man left in the family, I suppose.'

'Yes, and he wanted to act like a man with me but he couldn't get over being her child still.'

What was his mother like, I asked. She answered with the usual physical description. I insisted: 'As a person …'

'All right, I suppose. She's got a hard hand, that's for sure. When the old man was still alive, she didn't have much to say for herself. But once he was dead she took over. She once turned the señorita away from the farmhouse when she came looking for crops. "Whose home is this?" she said to her, barring the door. "Mine. And people only come in when I invite them." Of course, the señorita was hidden in the house during the war so she owed them a bit of respect. Not that she ever showed it, from what Miguel told me.'

'Isn't she a religious woman?'

'Yes. Well, she'll have learnt now. The second time round …'

'What do you mean?'

Surprised that I didn't know, she described how, on Miguel's father's death of a heart attack, the priest refused to bury him in holy ground because he hadn't received absolution. Miguel pleaded with the priest to no avail. At last he said: 'My father was more devout than any of those you see crossing themselves in church today – they were all Reds.' The priest took the point: it was well known that his own father had been one of those 'Reds'.

'Did Miguel ever talk to you about Antonio?'

'No, he never mentioned him. I can remember him because he was a friend of my father's, he used to come to our house often when I was a child. They were in the same thing together, you know what I mean. Antonio was lucky unlike – '

The garden gate opened and she stopped, bending over the Aga, clattering saucepans, as Bughleigh came up the path. Smooth and pink, his face appeared round the door. Sober, affable, he showed me out of the kitchen, apologizing for his absence and insisting that I have a drink. We had to go out to look at his latest gadget for watering roses, at the sundial he was making, a horse he'd just bought. A tour of the domain. He was delighted I'd come, I must have a swim, stay for lunch ... Loneliness exaggerated the insistence in his voice, the futility of his attempts to find something to keep himself engaged ... Is this what's going to happen in Benalamar one day?

When I got back I wrote Bob a note: 'Think the problem's solved, Bughleigh will put up the money. Leave it to you. Best, John.'

28

Later

Further jottings: indications.

Twin aims: Land: contesting the general fate, abstracting himself from María Burgos's domain, Miguel's project (at last confirmed) was to secure what few have achieved: a farm of his own. Marriage: transcending the area of least personal confidence, he attempted to secure, in Juana, the self-assurance of a wife. Money made both possible; and was made possible by his success as a farmer. Whatever its origins, his obsessive saving became part of a conscious project; careful of money, he was simultaneously carefree of time and trouble, a good neighbour.

Inter-related aims: establishing himself in the two vital areas of life, he would secure self-sufficiency where there had always been lack: his own master of woman and land.

Two losses: instead of fusing, the aims became antagonistic: to be the master of one he must renounce the other. This summer the two broke irremediably apart, in Juana's refusal to act the role, in María Burgos's refusal to act anything but the role; each betrayed him.

Or so he might have conceived it. Suddenly prepared, in an apparent reversal, to splash everything on a bracelet, repaying them by a show of success, imitating the rich, the foreigner.

Fatal flaws: Taking the blame for the betrayal on himself, as though he were its cause. Guilt. A man's man – joking and laughing – he wasn't 'man' enough to 'talk' to a woman; the head of the family was still a boy in his mother's eyes. Inadequacy. The child who was split, the adolescent whose future was decided for him. Rage. The young man who angrily projected goals to prove his adequacy as a man. Fetishization. The man who came so close to realizing those aims that their loss was the insufferable loss of himself. Despair. Inadequacy, guilt, rage turned back on themselves …

Speculations, that's all. If they were true, one would have to know why they were true.

Tomorrow, I'll try to find Ana.

29

22 September

Irony, they say, is the soul of modernism, though I think of
it rather as the hidden tension between the thing before and
after it's known. Pavese knew a thing or two about irony. A
writer and poet who became a Communist in the anti-fascist
struggle of the 1930s, he never believed he was a good enough
Communist. Mussolini, however, believed in his Communism
and dispatched him to internal exile. Too fine a writer to
believe in 'socialist art', too critical an intellectual to believe
in the inexorable progress of history, he nonetheless remained
a Communist. Lonely, uncertain of himself, he was desperate
for a lasting relationship with a woman. But the only profound
relationship he ever enjoyed was with his native Piedmont (how
often he compares its soft, smooth hills to women's breasts!).
Finally, a few years ago, he fell in love with an American actress.
The love wasn't returned and he committed suicide ...

   Why am I saying this? Because today that hidden tension
snapped and left me defenceless. Even the 'known', it turns out,
was not sufficiently known ... Perhaps nothing is ever definitively known and the irony ... But I'm intellectualizing to put
off the moment, delay it. This is how it happened.

   From the pine hill I saw Ana alone on the terrace below.

Unsure whether I could face the two women together, I'd hoped to find her without her mother. The time when I used to wait for her on the path where I was standing now seemed like another era. She was wearing black except for her straw hat – a dust-stained black dress that was too small and made her look childish, gawky somehow. A dog jumped up from her feet and came barking at me, churning up the dust.

I stopped a few yards away. 'Good afternoon.'

'Buenas tardes.' Her voice expressed the usual indifference and she barely looked at me.

'I've been meaning to come down before to say how sorry I am.'

'Sorry! It makes no difference. Everything is over.'

'Yes, I know. If I had known before …'

Her lips opened to say something, then she looked away. I felt she was about to reproach the banality of my condolences. What was it she wanted to say?

'Nothing. It's all over.' She stooped, felt for a stone and flung it underarm over the dry earth.

'Ana, one day things will be different.'

'No! How can they be with him gone! You can't understand. All the years he suffered and worked …'

'For what, Ana?'

'Why do you ask when you already know?'

'To buy a farm, wasn't it?' As I stepped towards her she moved back, as though to stay out of reach.

'I told my brother –'

'That's what he wanted, wasn't it, Ana?'

'What difference does it make to you, señorito, if my brother wanted land, if he was going to buy the farm?'

'Is that what he'd always wanted?'

'Always. Always, since he was young in the sierra. There weren't any foreigners then.' Her eyes, the irises almost as dark as the pupils, stared with anger. Let it pass, I thought, keep her talking.

'So it was in the mountains that he first had that dream. He never changed?'

'No. Not even when the foreigners came.' Now the dog, fangs showing, seemed to sense what she was feeling and slid forward from her feet.

'But he had other plans, too, didn't he?' I said, ignoring the dog. I wasn't going to let her escape. 'Juana, I mean.'

'That girl wasn't important to him.' Abruptly, she turned away. 'He was too good for her.'

'Maybe. But he wanted to marry her, didn't he?'

'My Miguel wouldn't have married her. She only wanted him for his money. To have a good time in the town. She's without shame.'

'She was the only woman he ever approached, Ana.'

'What do you mean?' Her hand went to her face and a smudge appeared under her eyes which were staring into the distance.

'I mean, he didn't find it easy to talk to a woman, did he?'

'He didn't want to. He was happy as he was.'

'He tried to see her those last nights.'

'Because she's shameless. She came to El Mayorazgo to make trouble for him. My mother told him he didn't need a woman like that. We gave him all he needed, all.'

The motherly love, sisterly devotion, domestic comfort, without having to leave the family, I thought. Softly, I said: 'Ana, do you remember once when I came down and Miguel was showing me how to drink from the pitcher? Or another afternoon perhaps, and he argued with you ...'

'Ay! Why do you come down here to remind me of this?' Gulping, her eyes filled with tears and she buried her head in her hands.

'Ana, I only meant –'

She sprang away from my touch.

'I loved him. I didn't betray him … I knew everything he was thinking. I loved him so much. I couldn't do anything.'

'What was there to do?'

'No! You could have …'

My head started to drain.

'You don't know what you did! You, señorito!'

'But Ana, the job, the water – I tried …'

'No, the land. Tío Bigote's. He wouldn't sell at the price.'

'I don't understand.'

'Tío Bigote's!' she screamed. 'He put the price up for you. Miguel hadn't the money.'

'What are you talking about?'

'You were looking for land, everyone said so. Tío Bigote's is the only farm you could buy. Why else were you always coming down here?'

Oh Christ, I thought. 'I came down to see Miguel, you …'

Her tear-stained eyes showed no sign of belief. Guilt turned into anger: 'Who said I was looking for land?'

'Everyone. That's what the foreigners want.'

'Ana, who?'

'Culebra saw you talking with Tío Bigote. Antonio Ríos, too, he was dealing for him.'

'Antonio Ríos,' I said, remembering the middleman who negotiated Bob's purchase of land, and his casual remark one day in the bar: there's a good farm, Sr John, down in the hills going cheap. Ah, I replied, which one is that? I'll take you down, you'll see … Just then Bob appeared and I never gave the matter another thought.

'Why didn't Miguel tell me, Ana? I could have explained. I've never tried to buy land.'

'My brother asked favours of no one, he had too much respect. You had money to buy …'

{154}

'Respect! Respect that leads to this! My God, he came to ask for work on the dam. You know that, don't you?'

'No!' For the first time she looked me in the eye. 'No, he came to ask about Tío Bigote's land, but he couldn't bring himself to it …' Again I saw Miguel diffidently standing by the granary door while I looked at him indifferently. 'I begged him to see you, tell you what was happening. When he came back he said he'd asked you for work. He was ashamed to ask favours he couldn't return.' Watching me scrabbling to pick up the typewritten sheets the gust of hot wind blew on the floor around his feet. Bending down himself to help gather these incomprehensible bits of paper, leaving with my faint promise to ask Bob for a day-labourer's job on the dam.

'There's been a terrible mistake, Ana. I never spoke to Tío Bigote or anyone else about buying his farm.'

But she was too distraught to listen. 'Why did you keep coming down, señorito, why? Making trouble for my brother.'

'Trouble?' Walking, talking, watching – nothing else. A way to spend the hot afternoons …

'That was all he wanted,' she cried. 'His own farm – and you …'

'I understand, yes.' But other things also had happened. The water drying up, the señorita's refusal to allow a channel across her land …

'With good crops this year my brother would have had the extra money he needed. I know, he told me.'

'That's what I mean.'

For once she didn't immediately answer. Suddenly she raised her eyes from the ground and said: 'So you should know, señorito, what you did. When the water flowed to waste he went over there' – pointing in the direction of the watercourse below the new borehole – 'and threw himself in it. I pulled him out. I think he meant to drown himself.'

I shuddered. The fever in my head was rising, I feared I might not last out. Defensively, I said: 'If the señorita had agreed promptly to the channel across her land Miguel would have had water. You know that.'

'What difference would it have made? Tío Bigote knew that a foreigner would pay more. Like your friend. And with the dam ...'

'The dam?'

'Of course. Don't you understand. Antonio Ríos told Tío Bigote to wait until the dam was finished. You'd be sure then to pay an even better price.'

'And that's why, I suppose, your mother put in charges against the dam.'

'Yes.' Moving back, defiant. 'Yes, you and the other foreigner will never finish it now.'

'Is that what Miguel would have wanted, Ana?'

'Yes, yes. He had no confidence in it.'

'He never told me.'

'Why should he?' She was implacable, unyielding. 'He didn't want trouble. All he wanted was for us to live in peace.'

'You call this peace? This fight with the land, the landlord, the water. Your older brother, Antonio, wouldn't have called this peace, I'm sure.'

It was perhaps desperation that drove me so far. She moved towards me, her face contorted and her arm raised as though about to strike out.

'None of this would have happened if ...' she hissed.

'Yes, go on.'

'If you hadn't come. We would have been free of the señorita, free of everyone.' And a despairing exultation rose in her cry.

30

23 September

Can one believe that by the mere fact of existing one can make land prices rise? By the mere fact of walking of an afternoon in the countryside shatter someone's life? That doing nothing, just being, could have such undreamt-of consequences? Is this the ultimate irony of indifference? An indifference I took to be sufficient protection against being identified as a *foreigner*, wealthy and land-seeking, the foreigner Bob is. Plainly, it wasn't enough. Indifference, I suppose, never is.

They – who exactly? – used a foreigner for their own ends, I believe. Or rather, they used my refusal to define myself clearly for purposes I never intended. A foreigner's afternoon walks weren't innocent, were they? My interest in the land was open to other interpretations than my own. My friendship with Bob put me in the same bag. Miguel must have shared their view. The irony of the known that remains unknown: even the most intimately known – oneself.

Is it exaggerated, nonetheless, to see María Burgos behind all this? Perhaps. But if she wanted to keep Miguel on her land, prevent him from realizing his dream, she and her agents could not have found a better accomplice than me.

This morning I thought of leaving Benalamar immediately.

The idea came after eighteen hours in bed, where I collapsed on returning from Ana's. But I have the feeling now that, *their* purpose having been achieved, my leaving or staying is immaterial. The terrible damage has been done, and it can't be undone. I shall stay: to write about Miguel.

IV. Miguel

31

A sudden effulgence, like the soundless flare from a cannon's mouth, gave him plenty of warning: a quarter of an hour at least before the car, whose roof blazed in the sun as it emerged on this side of the hills, reached the village. Standing in the cave he watched the black speck trailing dust far below. The inspectors! Miguel prepared to trot down to the olive mill (only in the last stretch did he run), but first he narrowed his eyes against the winter sun. The last but one car to make its slow way up the road had been not the inspectors but a taxi with men clinging to the roof and running boards; on the point of leaving his lookout too soon, he'd almost failed to see them. His heart beat with fear: the ragged men returning from the war, the war on the other side, had clambered from the roof and poured out of the taxi by the time he pushed his way through the crowd, anxiously searching among them for a face. Round the taxi, mothers and wives were crying at the sight of their men, touching them unbelievingly: the men who'd fled the village in time to get to the other side, their side which suddenly had no longer been here but *there* in another world unimaginable to Miguel beyond the mountains.

Antonio wasn't among the returning soldiers. The hope beyond hope that Miguel slowly learned to forget as he wandered in search of pasture for the goats had returned in the long, fruitless hours on the lookout for a car. He turned away from the frightening homecoming, seeing (as the wailing women had seen) the casual but well-known spectators who'd gathered at a slight distance to watch in silence. By that evening not one of the returned men was at home with his family; and by the following morning most were on their way back to mass court-martials in the town.

When Antonio returned, it wouldn't be like this; he'd walk through the night. The branch of the fig rustling against the closed shutter of the granary where they shared a bed … Rustle, tap three times, rustle again … It was the signal he awaited, unbelievingly and yet certainly: and the night it came he'd creep silently down, past the room where his father snored and Ana gave little cries in her sleep and his mother's eyes, he imagined, were watchfully awake, and step outside. There he'd be! Joyously, he'd run into his open arms.

Time and again in the lonely cave he imagined the scene as Antonio clasped him, then broke away, slapping him on the back. 'Miguelito! How you've grown! You're a man now!'

A shiver of pride ran down his back under his brother's hand. 'Everything's ready in the cowshed, Antonio,' he said, trying to hide the tremor in his voice. 'Father doesn't know.'

'Well, what was good enough for her will be good enough for me,' he laughed. But first he wanted to know everything that had happened since he left. Gravely, as though in his brother's absence he had assumed his gravity but not his joy, Miguel told him: the echoing shots by the boulder the night he left, the men returning now, the señorita's charges against him …

'So that was her thanks! Do you remember the night you saw her?' Miguel nodded. How well he remembered! – without remembering whether it was a dream or had really happened. 'I couldn't tell you, you were still a child. You might have said something somewhere. And that would have been the end of her – and maybe me too!'

At the beginning there'd been such commotion, so much confusion, so many men coming and going with newly seized weapons – shotguns and old pistols and even a sabre taken from one of the landlords' houses – that the slow-turning world seemed to have been stood on its head. Antonio, at the heart of the unknown, vanished – helping to reduce the Guardia Civil barracks, he later found out – leaving Miguel, excited and frightened, in this crazily spinning world. Armed men patrolled the countryside, requisitioned crops; landlords disappeared; the gutted church became the collective's warehouse ... Monolithically aloof, his father continued as though nothing were happening, while (to the boy's dismay) his mother's anxiety was all too evident.

On one of those first nights before Antonio returned, Miguel was woken by noises from the cowshed which abutted onto the house. He listened: low voices, an object dully falling, the scuffle of feet and sacks being moved. Frightened, he pulled the thin blanket round his head.

When his father went out early the next morning and he was alone with his mother, he told her what he'd heard. His mother was as close to him as his father was distant; he loved her without fear and she loved her youngest son with an indulgence she had had little enough time to express in the years before Carmela died. She demanded nothing of him except that he remain her child – a child she always feared losing. In the name of my love, love your dependence on me, she might have said had she ever thought of expressing their relationship in words.

Her sharpness was more shocking for being unaccustomed.

'You didn't hear anything. You were dreaming.'

'But ...'

'You heard nothing,' she repeated, even more sharply. 'Nothing.'

For a moment he was silenced; then, fully aware of the risk he was running, he said: 'I heard voices.' He saw the fear and anger on her face. The next moment her hand hit out and he reeled back.

'Stupid!' she shouted. 'Never, ever, another word about it – to anyone, do you understand? You'll bring them down on us if you do.'

Her terror sank him in a chasm without foothold. Unwillingly, he'd made her suffer, brought danger to the house. He went out and wandered alone. Was his mother capable of such betrayal of love?

The cowshed door was now kept firmly shut and he gave it a wide berth. At home he noticed a new tension; only Antonio in his brief moments there was his usual confident self. Even their father, so apparently in control of himself, seemed always on the alert. These were fearsome times.

Who could say then why his need to pee one night took him to the cowshed instead of the privy on the other side of the house. Half asleep, he heard a muffled cry and stumbled into her squatting figure; a hand grabbed his leg: 'Ssshh … who are you?' He was too terrified to answer. 'Miguelito?' He nodded soundlessly. 'Come here,' the voice whispered. 'Come close.' She had her hand on his neck and he had no choice. 'Do you know who I am?' He shook his head; but he thought he recognized the voice. Without a word she pulled him into the muggy cowshed where, to his surprise, he saw a long, deep pit, lit by an oil taper, beneath the fodder rack. A plank and sacks of dried maize had been pushed aside. The bottom was covered by a cotton mattress.

The flickering flame, hidden from outside, threw grotesque shadows over the sleeping cows' flanks and on her face.

'Now do you know who I am?'

'Yes, señorita ...' He recognized only her face; the rest of her was disguised by a farmworker's trousers and shirt, her hair cut short like a man's. He shivered despite the heat.

'Miguelito,' she began softly, 'your father is a good man. He is on our side. You must respect him always.' She looked at him intently, still holding him by the neck. 'On our side,' she repeated, 'the side of law and order. Do you understand?'

'Yes, señorita.'

Suddenly her voice changed. 'Whose farm is this?' she asked abruptly. He didn't reply quickly enough and he felt her tighten her grip on him.

'Don Gil, your father, señorita.'

'And what did your brother and his cowards do to him?'

Miguel didn't dare answer.

'What did they do?' She shook him ferociously with both hands. 'They killed him – an innocent old man – for nothing. Nothing. What did he ever do to them? Nothing. And they shot him in cold blood like the criminals they are.'

The shadows flickered over her face and her eyes gleamed. And then Miguel saw they had filled with tears. She wiped them away brusquely.

'Now do you understand why you mustn't listen to your brother? He is a bad man like them all. And God will have his vengeance on them when order is restored. For the godless cannot win a crusade, the godless who assassinate and burn churches.'

For a moment Miguel recalled that frightening moment in the square where people were throwing statues, pews, vestments – anything that would burn – onto the bonfire they'd just lit. Drifts of smoke came from the church but there was little or nothing inside that would catch. He imagined his mother standing where he was, desolate, throwing herself on her knees weeping. An overwhelming sense of sin took hold of him: a collective desecration whose sin was his own by the sole fact of witnessing it. Guilt drained him of all feeling except a bloodied hollowness inside.

He looked at the señorita mutely. Antonio was suddenly standing on the fountain shouting at the people that they were doing wrong, telling them to stop. The guilt was washed back to its hidden source by a wave of pride. His Antonio was saying what *he* felt: ordering the people to end all this wrong-doing. But it was useless; men pointed their guns at him and told him to leave. Doing right was rewarded with wrong.

'Who owns El Mayorazgo now?'

He was silent.

'The señorita owns it, it is mine,' she said triumphantly. 'My father – may his soul rest in peace – set it aside for me as a young girl. I was the only one who accompanied him every-where, for whom the land meant anything. It is mine – and it's going to stay mine as long as I live.'

She too was silent now, but her eyes never left his. Her presence mesmerized him.

'Your brother thinks he is going to take this, take all the farms from me – the "land for those who work it" he tells the people who are too ignorant to know better. I tell you he won't.' So great was the vehemence in her voice that she seemed to have Antonio in front of her instead of a child. 'Now you know why you must never listen to your brother. He is a criminal.'

Then, as though aware of danger, her tone lowered. 'But you are a good boy, nearly a man. You'll be working soon. One day, if you take after your father, as you must, you may work this land for me as he did for my father. But for that you must forget you saw me. It is a dream. I'm not here, never have been.'

As rapidly as he'd been pulled into the cowshed, a sharp push in the back expelled him.

In their bed Antonio was snoring gently. Miguel touched, shook him but he wouldn't wake up. At first light, Antonio was already pulling on his trousers, stooping so as not to hit his head on the cane ceiling. Miguel was about to tell him when something held him back. Inevitably, his brother would ask what she'd said; how could he tell him?

'Time to get the goats out.' Antonio leant over the bed to tap him on the shoulder. 'I'm off to the collective. Tell our mother for me.' Then he was gone and it was too late. Miguel kept the monstrous secret, unaware that his brother was doing everything in his power to save her; nor in the years to come, when the señorita's prophecy came true, did he ever refer to that terrifying night.

But as he wandered in search of pasture he tried to make sense of this contradictory world. Who was right, who wrong? The señorita frightened him, but her words about his brother he rejected with instinctive outrage. Antonio was his companion of childhood. But then there was his father who had turned on Antonio in blind anger at his son's insistence that El Mayorazgo become part of the collective. Their father rose from the table, his hand went to his belt as though Antonio were a boy he could still thrash, and he ordered him out of the house.

'I shall go,' Antonio replied calmly, 'when I've finished my supper. There are more important things happening here, and all over Spain, than depend on a single man's ...'

His father's hand crashed on the table, crashed through Miguel. 'This Republic of yours is responsible for what has happened. Now go!'

'It's no Republic of mine!' Antonio looked up from his plate. 'But now we workers hold power, there's the difference.'

His father glowered at him, at Miguel too lest, the boy felt, he was siding with his brother. 'A son doesn't argue with his father,' he said in a voice that might have been engraved in stone. And then he walked out of the house.

The assured world of familiar duties and respect collapsed round Miguel's ears. Antonio went on eating as though nothing had happened, his mother sitting opposite him stunned beyond words. Miguel yearned suddenly to run after his father to reassure him that he was not part of this betrayal. For only a few days earlier his father had entrusted him for the first time with a task that gave him a place in the world. Leading in the few goats left from the original herd he'd had to sell, he looked at Miguel as though seeing him for the first time other than as a child.

'Tomorrow you take the goats to pasture. You're man enough now for that.'

His heart leapt, but he said nothing. His father didn't need unnecessary words. Soon after dawn the next morning he had the goats out and set off for the best pasture; these bleating, butting animals would be the living proof that he merited his father's trust and repaid it, wordlessly, with respect.

So where was the good, where the bad? He remembered his joy when, in the square, Antonio furled him in the red and black neckerchief, remembered the times when his brother took him by the hand and they went looking for insects and small animals on the terraces by the house. 'Look at that snail,' he'd say before Miguel had seen it. 'See how perfect the shell is.' He ran his finger over the polished case. 'That's how nature is, perfect, everything in its place. It's only us who can't match nature.' His brother who knew everything and shared it with him, his companion who was closer to him than his father. But Antonio frightened him too, by his defiance, for always the boy feared that the punishment to come would fall on him; he was too small to stand up to the patriarch who could be won over only by silent and dutiful respect. He felt (and always would feel) a sense of inadequacy: the impossibility of standing against the world like his brother or, like his father, of towering above it.

In the solitude of the day, Miguel was happy yet joyless. The civil war drew its lines through the home and ran through him. His father and brother no longer spoke to each other; his mother, racked by anguish, passed on the little that each had to say. The unspoken, hidden presence in the cowshed was a permanent threat which, unknown to him, his mother had used to patch up this fragile truce.

'If it wasn't for Antonio, the militiamen would be here every day as they are at Matanzas and El Vicente,' was her reproach to her unbending husband in private. 'They'd find the señorita, be sure of that. Your son is our protection, salvation … I pray to the Virgin every night for him. And you – you want to drive him out.' Though he refused to recognize the first words of criticism she had ever addressed to him, he never again tried to force his son from the house. Other events would soon bring that about.

Caught in the silent cross-fire, Miguel fell silent too; the conflict of loyalties paralysed him. Split between father and brother, he felt threatened and helpless. Nubs of anxiety swelled on the underside of his muteness: soon he came to believe that each was silently censuring him for his betrayal, the failure to give total allegiance. Guilt flowed along the battle lines drawn through his heart. He'd been found wanting in the eyes of men.

Crouched in the shade of an olive, his sling to hand, he knew that even this new place in the world depended each night on his father's glance when he brought in the small herd. Silence was the only praise he could expect; a curt word or two would prove his inadequacy. He braced himself; approval lay in that silent gaze. He had to succeed – and succeed as the man his father expected: he looked after the goats as though his life depended on them. If that meant stealing a bit of fodder here or there, he was ready to do it. The goats had never looked so good. Little by little, as the lack of reproof confirmed his success, he became less fearful of the evening return. But he was never entirely free of anxiety: the struggle to prove himself was always undermined by the fear of failing. And what he had won during the day served for nothing in the conflict of loyalties by night.

The rumble of artillery behind the mountains was soon heard. He knew – Antonio didn't hide it from him – that the enemy was advancing. Antonio said they would fight to the end; the trenches being dug on the village slopes were the proof. Franco had been at the gates of Madrid for over two months and the capital still resisted. But when one cold February dawn the enemy attacked from the least expected direction, Miguel saw the frightened militiamen fleeing from the mountains to avoid being cut off; all the efforts of Antonio and the other trade union leaders could not stop them.

That evening, late, Antonio came home exhausted. What he said to his parents Miguel never knew. What he said to him, waking him up, Miguel never forgot: 'The struggle here is over, Miguelito. Tomorrow the fascists will arrive. But this isn't the end – it's only the beginning ...' The big cities, he went on, were anti-fascist strongholds, elsewhere the landworkers had a greater revolutionary spirit than those in Benalamar, the fruit of harsher struggles. The anarcho-syndicalist columns on the Aragon front and in Madrid were strong. 'The revolution will triumph. But until then I have to leave you to fight with our companions.' He took hold of his hand as he used to when Miguel was small. 'You're too young to come with me. It breaks my heart that you'll have to live under the fascists. But it won't be for long. Nothing will happen to you, but my life is in danger. I want to fight – and die if I have to – face to face with the enemy. If I don't come back, Miguelito, you'll know that I died for what

I believe in. Not our father's belief in the landlord's rights, no, but the right of every worker to the land that he works.'

'But you'll come back, Antonio, won't you?'

'Yes, Miguelito, when our revolution triumphs, I hope so.'

'You'll come back and I'll be waiting for you …' Suddenly the image came to the boy's mind: 'And you'll tap three times on the shutters with the branch of the fig and I'll know it is you.'

'Yes. I'll climb the tree and tap.'

'Three times, Antonio. I'll be waiting. I'll let you in.'

'Yes. Now go back to sleep.'

When he awoke Antonio had gone; and he knew in his heart that he would never return.

32

As he reached the square he broke into a run: no one would say he wasn't a good look-out for the eight pesetas he earned a day. He'd been doing it for three years, and the trot down from the cave was welcome, taking his mind off his empty belly; up in his solitary outpost he could never forget the hunger. Three bitter years since the war ended and a Red Cross telegram, which the town hall clerk read to his father, broke the news which his father passed on without comment, as though he had considered Antonio dead since the day he left. For days Miguel hadn't believed it. Antonio had promised! Only his mother's staunchless flow of tears convinced him. Somewhere, in the nebulous regions of the soul, his anger at Antonio's original flight returned. His brother had abandoned him: left him to stare alone at the blood-stained boulder, left him among those who would, if they could, have shot him. Thank God, something told him, Antonio had escaped; but when José, his goatherding companion, taunted him with Antonio's flight, the rage rose destructively from deep inside: Antonio would never come back, he didn't want him back. Antonio had failed him.

The rage brought guilt. Secretly he prepared the señorita's hiding place in the cowshed, knowing that Antonio would need it. How could he want his brother's obliteration? Miguel wanted nothing more than his brother's return.

With the news of his death on the Ebro, the rage was more intense. From the lookout post, the sling cracked in the air and stones ricocheted and clattered down the side of the hill. Deadly bullets. Rocks, scraggly rosemary, thyme, died in the hail. Why had he trusted him? His arm turned in a frenzy, spewing stones into the sun. Who was he trying to kill? Anyone, everyone … His brother's killers … In the bedrock beneath awareness lay fear: had his own rage killed Antonio? Obliterated him? Suddenly, without knowing why, he flung the sling to the back of the cave and began to cry. The terrible loss was too grievous. Antonio was never coming back.

For weeks he lived in a greyness from which he couldn't rouse himself. He sat in the cave staring unseeingly at the road below. The señorita, the inspectors, were unimportant: he'd sat there these months waiting, hope against hope, for Antonio; stayed awake at night waiting for the tap, tap, tap on the shutters. Days and nights were shaped, given meaning by hope. And now there was nothing.

33

Three years of peace, three years of drought. Few escaped the hunger now. Bursting through the olive mill's door he shouted: 'A car! The inspectors!' The foreman grabbed the donkey pulling the millstone. Labourers leapt on the wicker baskets of olives and barrels of oil and carried them to their underground hiding place. Miguel knew his next task: to run down the track to turn back the sharecroppers bringing up olives on their donkeys. The señorita's mill had an official quota of oil it could produce for the village alone. But at night the lorries left with black-market barrels for the town, leaving only the rancid last crushing for the village.

This particular morning the señorita was in the mill. Before Miguel rushed off again, she caught him for a moment with her eyes: 'Good boy!' they said. He asked nothing more of her. But his eyes were blank.

When he'd finished warning the sharecroppers, he made himself scarce; the rest of this business had nothing to do with him. He was hungry, had been hungry for so long that he'd forgotten what it was like to have a full stomach. When, each evening, he laid his day-wage on the table he knew there was nothing it would buy; the village shops were empty. At home they were down to the last half-sack of maize, and even if it rained they wouldn't be able to plant because no seed corn was left. He longed for Easter when his mother would make him and Ana the only egg they tasted all year – an egg which curdled his weak stomach and sent him out the back to vomit. Every other day of the year his mother took the eggs down to Torre del Mar to exchange on the black market for whatever she could find; that was all that was keeping them alive.

Was this what the war and the killing had been for? Was this why Antonio had died? So that everyone except the señorita and a few others should starve?

That evening his father stopped him by the door. 'Son, tomorrow you go to your uncle's in the sierra. Be ready at noon.' He turned on his heel without another word.

There was no time to say anything. Miguel was stunned. He saw a man on a donkey climbing the track, a woman in black following him, and then the land slid away, fell from him. Familiar objects stood out in misty separation, a posed isolation disconnected them from him. His guts drained. It suddenly seemed as though he didn't exist, as though he were a child again. Everything that had been gained, the small prominence he had believed secure, disintegrated; the loss was a part of him that had been ripped out.

What had he done to deserve this?

Stocky and silent, his uncle walked ahead; there was too much suffering, too much pain to take heed of a boy's drawn face, his hurt. He would learn soon enough that he was in luck. The old man let his mind empty, become as blank as the vault of the sky; it was no use thinking, no use feeling, nothing would be changed by it.

The boy plodded behind. It was a five-hour walk along mule tracks to the farm, which lay in a fold on the side of the mountains. Soon they passed the limits of Miguel's wanderings and he held back his tears. The gnarled olives pointed, reminded him of his loss, and he wanted to turn and run home. But in his mother's tearful eyes he had seen acceptance, defeat. Momentarily he hated her for what she had agreed to, rejected her for not siding entirely with him; and then, finding that he was rejecting the one person he loved, that without her the loss was insuperable, his guilt overwhelmed him and he hated himself. Everything turned back on him. Unsure of his right to exist, he recognized himself in his insufficiency. How else to explain the loss but to blame himself?

They reached the farmstead at dusk; his uncle had said barely a couple of words and, with not many more, he sent the boy out the next morning with the herd. Up on the mountainside the loss was confirmed: the village had vanished as completely as if it had never existed. He began to cry. No one would hear or know or care. An absence torn from himself, he was no more to anyone than a boulder, a stone, an object as inanimate as the mountain itself. He lay on a rock and cried for a long time.

When, at last, he half-opened his eyes he saw the herd had spread over the mountainside. He scrambled after the goats, numb and yet fearful that something might have happened to one of them, incapable of escaping even this sense of failure. Wildly, he hurled stones at them from his sling and, as the herd reassembled and he saw that his absence had not caused a disaster, began to take relief in the movement of his arm, the accuracy of his aim. For the rest of the day he kept himself from looking behind where the few isolated farmsteads, white in the distant hills, reminded him of what he no longer could see, and kept the herd moving towards the summit.

He returned to the farmstead that night and for a few nights more until his uncle was satisfied; then he was told to take the herd on its summer migration. He left the lonely cottage without regret except for the food which was plentiful. The farmstead was irrigated and his uncle was selling his wheat on the black market while his sons were busy on contraband deals. It was a family richer than Miguel's, which could well afford to keep him as a poor relative without pay. But its small comforts were no substitute for the home and the village he had lost; without them it was a matter of indifference where he was.

He set out one dawn knowing he wouldn't return until the autumn, three months away. In the high mountain passes, where there was still grass, the sun burnt down by day and at night it was cold. Wrapped in a skin, he slept huddled among the goats, barely distinguishable from the packed herd. Following the goats in the heat of the day, he kept up at first a self-recriminatory monologue; but after a time even that dried and his mind became baked, hard as the volcanic rock of his surroundings, and it was only in dreams that he rediscovered his loss.

There was no future. Had he thought that this life would continue another two years, he might have revolted. But instead of the future there existed only the past, the past as the future for which he yearned. A return to what he had known. Another of his age might have assumed that this exile was evidence of the past's irrecuperable ending and sought to escape what had rejected him. He waited. It was always this way: the intimate meaning came from outside. Things happened, others decided and his life was made. He waited for the magical appearance of his father on the rocky skyline one day to call him home as inexplicably as he'd sent him away and there to receive forgiveness. Even this numbed expectation dried up at last.

Instead it was another goatherd who appeared one morning and who stood there, as immobile as a rock, staring at him. In surprise, Miguel threw up his arms and began to run forward; then, remembering himself, he walked slowly, gravely towards the man. He saluted the goatherd, from whose matted hair sharp eyes peered at him. The man made a sound, a squeal. Not understanding, Miguel repeated his greeting; in reply, the goat-herd capered like one of his charges, pointing with his fingers at his head. A half-wit, Miguel realized, but it still took him some minutes to comprehend that his companion – the first human he had seen for two months – was also a deaf-mute. Better than nothing, Miguel thought, feeling the pull of unused muscles as he smiled; what else could one expect?

They let their herds graze in common and remained together the rest of the summer. Miguel grew attached to his companion, who lived with the ease of a goat in these barren mountains, who knew instinctively the best pastures to make for, who on a hungry impulse would slaughter a goat and roast it over a fire. They communicated by squeals and signs and occasional caperings and gradually, through the dusty dryness, the boy felt himself stirring: he was alive again, but in a different, animal-like way. One evening, seeing himself in a piece of glass the deaf-mute had found, he discovered he looked little different from his companion: matted hair and half-mad, cunning eyes staring out of a drawn, sullen face. All the next day Miguel refused the grunts and squeals and would only talk to his com-panion, who watched him suspiciously as though he had gone mad. But there was no alternative other than to set off alone again with the herd and he preferred a half-human compan-ionship to that unending solitude. Together they continued their voyage over those infinite wastes, their primitive contact unheard and unseen by anything living but the goats they so closely resembled, until the first frosts came and it was time to separate.

34

He had left his uncle's farmstead without regrets and returned to discover its comforts: food and a bed and people who talked. If it was not home it was second best. For the village fair he got a couple of days off, and ran most of the way home. The joy at being back was so great that he didn't immediately notice his family's reduced straits: hunger gripped them and his mother showed its effects. Miguel's experiences were distant to her. She chided him for his unkempt appearance without taking account of the reasons for it, and wept for him among many when she prayed for them all. She asked if he got enough to eat – what else was there to ask? – and he said yes, seeing the small ration of corn bread in her hand.

'Well, they have land and water of their own, they produce for their needs,' she said.

'More than that, for the black market as well.'

'Ay! The black market. The señorita and the mayor are making their fortunes, as though they needed it.'

His mother's despair was widely shared. He went back to the mountains heavy-hearted. He seemed to belong nowhere now. Either he or his home had changed too much for him to return to the past he had known; but his uncle's farmstead was not his home, he had no future there. Obscurely he came to realize one thing: he would not follow in his father's footsteps. He watched his uncle. Though the earth was poor, there was an abundance of water from springs in the mountain, and by working from dawn until nightfall, his uncle had paid for the farm in ten years. As taciturn as Miguel's father, he was a great deal shrewder, the nephew observed. He controlled everything, nothing was done without his command. Even the outlaws, when they came down in winter, accorded him their cautious respect, knowing they were dependent on prosperous peasants like him for their security and supplies. And he served his 'guests' with shrewd peasant eyes, knowing full well where his interests lay.

That spring Miguel asked his uncle to let him stay on the farmstead to work. The old man's eyes showed a moment's surprise at the audacity of the request. Then, angrily, he asked the boy what he thought he was there for, turning away before Miguel could speak. The dependency, in which charity replaced wages, was brutal enough for the boy to understand: it must be escaped one day.

Resentfully, when the time came, he took the herd off, not caring what happened to it, no longer expecting miracles. The barren mountains, the scattered herd under the transparent blue sky, reflected nothing – nothing of himself. He needed something to cling to, some goal intimately his own in whose realization he could imagine himself depending on no one, self-sufficient.

Nothing presented itself except the deaf-mute, with whom he joined up again. For a time he lost himself in prancing and squealing, glad of the company but always watching himself, aware of how little it took to sink to an animal-like state. He didn't want to see himself or be seen in that condition, and when one evening the men appeared, as though they had sprung from the ground, his fear was as much of his unmanly state as of their guns and rapid approach. He stood his ground while the deaf-mute fled. The men sent him to fetch his companion, and then ordered the two of them to slaughter several goats, prepared a fire and sat roasting the best cuts. It was evident they meant the goatherds no harm and Miguel sat with them, taking the contraband tobacco they were handing round. He looked at the grizzled, sun-beaten faces, thinking that some of them might have been at the farmstead, when one of them sprang out from some distant memory. The man caught his eye:

'Who are you, boy, where do you come from?' Miguel told him and the man laughed. 'Juan the goatherd's son, eh? Antonio's brother. From across the street ...'

Gaunter, older – an old man almost, it seemed – Fernando had been his brother's friend and companion. He moved round to Miguel's side and questioned him about the village, appearing to know as much if not more than Miguel had to tell. The other men were busy eating and teasing the deaf-mute who smiled and squealed.

'Antonio died for the revolution,' he said. 'You can be proud of him. He wasn't one of those who renounced their ideas.'

Miguel looked at him. Was that all there was? To be proud of his brother for getting killed with unchanged ideals? The old rage rose in him and he began to crack brushwood across his knee, throwing it on the fire. If Antonio had come back ...

'When he had the time he worked on the collectives behind the lines. That's where our revolution was consolidating, in the agrarian collectives. "This is the future made real," Antonio used to say.'

'There's only those with their own land and the falangistas who are getting rich now,' Miguel mumbled.

'And the priests ... But this lot won't last long. Look at what's happening to their German and Italian allies. They're losing the war to the Russians and Americans and when they do, things will change here.'

The flames flickered on Fernando's vulpine face; Miguel understood little of what he was saying: the second world war, the revolution that would spring to life once the fascists were gone ... Later, when the men vanished in the dark and the conversation turned in his head, he thought of his brother. Antonio could have been alive in these mountains, Antonio could have been talking to him.

The outlaws returned many times and when they didn't come Miguel and the deaf-mute slaughtered goats for themselves. From his companion Miguel learnt that the hides could be sold and every fortnight the boy set off for a village on the other side of the sierra. The money he shared with the deaf-mute, careful to hide his part in the lining of his coat where, at any moment, he could feel its satisfactory bulge. In those few worn, dirty notes he felt himself turned into worth; they made good the inadequacy he feared most in himself.

It was of the land and the landless that Fernando almost always spoke. For sharecroppers he had little but disdain: 'slaves of the landlord', they were frightened of progress. The real struggle lay between the few who owned much and the many who owned nothing but the force of their arms. 'And it was we, the labourers, who made the agrarian revolution ...'

The frosts came late, it was early winter before Miguel returned to his uncle's. There he had to explain the loss of a dozen goats, many of which he had killed himself. His uncle listened without a word to the boy's account of the outlaws ordering them to be slaughtered.

'The hides?' the old man asked sharply.

'They took them.' The lie was as transparent to his uncle as it was to him. But the old man turned away and it was never mentioned again.

All that winter, close by on the flanks of the sierra, he thought of escape from the mountains and goats. He imagined a world in which he would create what his father had failed to make. An obscure dream at first, little more than a feeling, it gradually took shape, the comforting, secure form of land, given reality by all he had heard. Antonio's voice spoke long-forgotten words in his ear: The land for those who work it ... Yes: a farmstead like his uncle's, only close to the village where he would prove himself worthy in the only way everyone understood: as a self-sufficient, independent, authoritative man.

This was an aim so distant, so abstract for a thirteen-year-old that it might have been impossible for another to sustain. But he, with his acute awareness of reality as belonging to others, must (if Ana is right) make such a leap – a flight – from reality into an imaginary world of his own. Out of the shadowy child-hood of insufficiency had emerged at last a choice that was his own, which would nullify the insufficiency that was its cause.

In the harsh years ahead, the years of day-labouring when there was work, the years of planting pines in the sierra, the aim would recede or he wouldn't have tried to escape by vol-unteering for the army. But when his father tore up the papers, confirming once more his powerlessness to decide his own future, he knew he was destined to sharecrop El Mayorazgo. The aim returned with force, as though indeed it had been waiting for him, and he rediscovered it with an *ah!* of surprise as the future's hidden meaning. Until the day Tío Bigote dropped the hint it remained a distant if definite aim; distant because its very importance to him would lead him to fear his inabil-ity to realize it; definite because, to overcome fear, he would forget in the course of the years that the aim had originated in him. To admit that the idea was his would entail admitting also that it was his to revoke – an arbitrary idea, tainted by his own inner sense of inadequacy. Instead, projected outside himself, it solidified like earth turning to stone, and returned to him as a demand that must be fulfilled. So the plough follows the line of the furrow that has already been inscribed in the earth. Until the day when it became a potential reality requiring him to act. Then the actual choice would reawaken the fear, the barely dormant self-doubt, fill him with anxiety that impeded decision, with guilt at this inability to act ... His 'idea', Juana said. His relationship to her was lived in much the same way as his attitude to the land.

Those times were still a long way ahead. As he came down the mountainside that winter evening, the decision was fresh in his mind. Without thinking, without noticing the silence, he locked the herd in the pen and went into the cottage. In no time, he staggered out and began to run, the fleeting picture engraved on his mind: his uncle, two cousins, his aunt hanging from the rafters with halters round their necks. He reached the next farmstead two miles away and babbled that the family had committed suicide; then he collapsed.

His father came for him and he was taken home. He had terrible nightmares and it was many days before anyone dared tell him the truth. The family had been killed by the outlaws who suspected the old man of betraying them to the Guardia Civil. His absence with the herd was all that had saved him.

35

John lay in bed later than usual. Miguel's childhood 'story' had poured out with such surprising rapidity that it had seemed to be waiting, already written, within him. The flow of words had continued uninterrupted until the end when, exhausted and unable to say where it had come from, he fell into bed. A sense of achievement accompanied his slow waking, his body aching as pleasantly as after a boyhood athletic triumph. At last, he thought sleepily, at last he'd accomplished what he'd set out to do! His passion to bring Miguel to life, the Miguel of childhood he'd never known, had been attained. Now there remained the Miguel he'd known.

Before long, as his mind focused, the satisfaction gave way to second thoughts: who could say whether the story accurately portrayed Miguel's childhood, was anything more than a fiction? The few known elements of Miguel's childhood had readily lent themselves to John's interpretation; but there was so little to go on that another interpretation could be equally valid. There was no way of knowing, of being sure, he thought uncomfortably.

But that, too, was inevitable: there'd always be more than one possible interpretation of any life, any event, he reassured himself. The reader would have to judge; he hadn't played at God, pretending to know more than the reader. No! No!

Everything that he'd learnt from his talks about Miguel had been noted down. Anyone could use these notes to propose a different interpretation, write a different account. More than that no writer could offer.

His slightly ridiculous anxiety made him laugh all of a sudden. A reader! And who would that be? He hadn't written his account to be read, and here he was vindicating it by invoking a mythical reader. It was laughable, even more so than his anxiety.

The laughter ended in waking him up fully. For a while he had been faintly aware of some change: now he distinctly felt that in place of the usual crystalline morning light there was a heaviness in the air. He got out of bed and, opening the shutters, the sensation was confirmed: a mass of cloud hung over the village. As he was looking at this unaccustomed sight, the first drop of rain fell. A single drop, as big as a marble, which hit the wall in front and streaked the whitewash a dusty red. Another gob splashed the cobbles. Soon large, isolated drops were banging on the roof and running down the walls, staining everything.

He ran downstairs shouting for Dolores. 'It's raining!' She was hurriedly bringing in the wash she had left out overnight.

'It's raining mud, that's what it's raining,' she said angrily, looking at the stained sheets. 'From the Sahara.'

'But it'll do the earth good.'

'No, it's a shower, nothing more.'

She was right; but the clouds didn't lift, and in the afternoon, on his way to the town hall for Bob's hearing, another shower caught him in the middle of the street. His face and shirt were streaked with drying desert dust as he took his place on a narrow bench next to Bob.

Opposite, so close he could have touched her, sat Miguel's mother staring stonily at the three men on the dais: the black-suited baker and Justice of the Peace (feeling for the matchstick stuck in the book at a page he'd spent time trying to find), a shopkeeper, and a man unknown to John. Her raisin-shrivelled face gave nothing away.

In a monotonous, almost incomprehensible voice, the baker read out the litigants' statements and counter-statements, thick fingers mistaking the pages, the voice continuing uninterrupted for a non-sequential sentence or two. Bob shuffled his feet, irked by the clumsy procedure; the two sharecroppers accompanying Miguel's mother sat open-mouthed on either side of her. She never moved.

There, within arm's length, was an I that had held secret desires and hopes for Miguel. There, in that skull, out of reach, lived memories of him. Her child. Always, until the end. Dependent on her. Transparent to her gaze. Unlike Antonio or Carmela, he was the one who had always needed her most …

John shook himself out of the fantasy. He wanted to tap those memories the way you'd tap a wine barrel, letting the past gush out of its own accord. She would never talk to him, that was sure. The argument of her case, even in the baker's monotone, was bitter: she accused Bob of not having secured the statutory permissions needed to construct the dam, and demanded that it be torn down as a public menace. Foreigners had no right to use their land to such a purpose … A heavy legal hand had patently drafted her case.

Had she seen Miguel's anxiety even before he was aware of it? Seen the self-doubt in his eyes and, deep beneath it, fear. Could he find the money? Would Tío Bigote take seven thousand? But he'd lose Juana if he stayed on the land. 'Son, think of yourself, think of us.' He wouldn't leave them for that woman and the town …

'Are the statements approved?' The baker looked at both

benches in turn. The crucifix over the dais seemed to ascend from his bald head between the Generalissimo's jowl and the dreamy profile of Antonio Primo de Rivera. Miguel's mother whispered to the man on her left, sat as though recasting everything in her mind, and said firmly:

'Yes.'

'Yes.' Bob's voice was a bit edgy.

The baker put a hand to the book in front of him, felt for the matchstick and opened it. He held the page for the shopkeeper and then for the unknown man to read. Both glanced at it cursorily. 'Yes, it is clear. It is as provided for,' said the baker closing the book. 'Yes. That is all. The hearing is concluded.'

'Concluded! But how?' Bob was on his feet. 'What is the verdict?'

'In due course, Sr Bob, it shall be made known.'

'But this is ridiculous.'

'It is as laid down. The proceedings are clear.'

'What about the work on the dam? Can it go on?'

'For the moment the matter rests as it is.'

'No!'

'The hearing is concluded. A report will be made.'

Miguel's mother got up.

'It's no use arguing, Bob,' John said.

'I've never heard anything so stupid. What sort of law is this?'

'Patience, it's a Spanish virtue.'

'Patience be buggered! I'm going to get my lawyers to come up and sort this lot out.' He shook off John's hand and stormed through the door into the bright sunlight that had replaced the Saharan clouds.

John followed him out. Miguel's mother had disappeared. He thought for a moment of sitting in the square to enjoy the freshness of the air. Instead, he took the side street that led to the threshing floor and the start of the track down to the hills; here no one would disturb him.

Seeing Miguel's mother had reminded John of how much he would never know. Could never know. Of her and Ana's hatred ...

There was nothing he could do except ignore it, push it to the back of his mind lest it interfered in some way with his obsession to finish writing. He had now to concentrate on Miguel at El Mayorazgo during these past months. On the self-inflicted death that seemed so futile at the time, but which he'd come to see as a conscious act, intelligible by what it sought to achieve: the attempt as in all human action to go beyond what exists even in the moment of destroying himself.

Such might be the logic of the process, John thought; but what had it meant to *Miguel* as he lived through those weeks and days?

36

Anxiety

Seven thousand ... Gushing down the channel, tentatively edging forward between the tomatoes, the water's flow sent a sense of well-being through him, easing the tension. It was a moment of rest, of coolness soaking the roots to be sucked into the freshly forming fruit, one of the few moments when the crop didn't need the weight of his hoe. What joy water brought! Through the trellis of canes the sun made an intricate pattern of shadow in which, like a ball spinning, the calculations revolved: two thousand five hundred, his share of the crop, if the water held. Five in the bank. Offer Tío Bigote seven, maybe he'll take seven and a half, no, it's worth more, but if the price of tomatoes drops this year ...

He sucked in his lower lip and stared at the water nudging forward, feeling its way, exploring the heat cracks, filling them, pushing on. May, only a month since he'd started irrigating and it was half last year's flow. He tried to order his thoughts, which, in the days since Tío Bigote spoke, had circled interminably, indecisively through him. Why couldn't he decide? There was the goal and he wanted it with an intensity so great that doubt proliferated like nettles in the over-fertile desire. Would the crop fetch as much as last year? Even if Tío Bigote took seven and half he'd have spent every last peseta saved, and what would there be to carry them through? His mother, Ana, what would they say? Juana? Nubs of anxiety formed. If he spent everything she'd have to wait … 'Always the land, Miguel, that's all you think of, that means more to you than getting married.'

Scooping up earth, his hoe changed the flow. The smell of wet earth rose to block off the heat, a curtain of freshness to which the plants added their pungent green smell. Every detail of Tío Bigote's farmstead that lay out of sight beyond the hill came to mind: seven good terraces, smaller than El Mayorazgo, but better for early tomatoes, enough land to raise a couple of calves, nothing to share. Good earth the old man had manured properly, unlike the señorita's farms, but he was getting too old, that's why he wanted to sell, he won't sell it cheap, not good land like that, he'll want more than seven and a half and with its own borehole – seven and a half, to get even that the water must hold. Pacing. Five in the bank, two and a half to find …

Was the old man already speaking to others, dropping the same hint – to others who wouldn't stare at him mumbling, 'So you'll be wanting to sell?' – letting him walk away, saying over his shoulder, 'When the offer's right,' and not even going to see him that night or the next.

His hand reached for the child's ruled notebook in his shirt pocket and thumbed the pages: five thousand *duros* for last year's crop, there in his own hand. Pleasure welled up: the crowd of neighbours come to watch the crates being loaded high on the lorry, the best price in Benalamar anyone could remember, the first time a lorry had come from Granada for a crop. 'And how about ours then?' some of the sharecroppers asked. With self-satisfaction concealed under the neighbourliness for which he was known, he spoke to the comprador for all of them except Tío Bigote, who stood on the edge and who, everyone knew, would go on loading his mule and selling the crop, basket by basket, day after day, in the village shops. But the comprador shook his head: none of the others' was early enough. He felt the men's eyes on him as they watched the notes being counted, placed in his hands, counted again. 'Hombre! You're making a fortune.' Pepe clapped him on the back.

'For the furniture,' he laughed, seeing Tío Bigote watching as he carefully folded the notes. He'd soon have enough for the nuptial bed and wardrobe, the chairs and table it was a man's duty to provide.

'Ay! When will it be?'

'This time next year. Maybe ...'

Ah, what would she say now to postponing it until who knew when? He watched her at the village fair swinging back and forth to the paso doble, hips swaying, heedless of gossip about the break with her betrothed. Easy – no, hombre, no; he didn't know how, never had. A writhing sense of longing that turned back on itself; he was better off as he was, mother, sister, no complications. A feeling of nearness, warmth that welled up from childhood: he and his mother, the others distant. The cornet blared out another paso doble and his eyes fixed on the swaying red dress, lost, reappearing in the crowd. Unnoticed these years, the girl suddenly become woman, unapproachable, different from others. Her eyes went boldly round the men; she would choose as she wanted, they seemed to say, she was free, sufficient to herself. Her difference tantalized him. Only a full-fledged man could be worthy of her ... On the way down the track in the dark, he'd laughed and joked with Pepe to cover the longing. 'Hombre, what you need is a woman,' Pepe laughed drunkenly. 'There's Juana, how about her?'

And she'd accepted him! The only woman he'd ever had the courage to ask! She'd be his wife. After three years he still couldn't believe it sometimes. It was a miracle and he was humbly grateful to be walking at her side; humble but also raised up that she – she! – should have accepted him. In her eyes was reflected his self-validation, but her eyes … they danced, they flashed, then the next evening they were dark and still.

'The land again, Miguel, what does it produce? Nothing but trouble. The weather is bad, there's not enough water, always something. And the señorita, look what she takes.'

No, no, she mustn't talk of the señorita like that, it's her farm, her right. And he told her about the terraces just seeded, the crop just sold, and she looked around to see who was walking out with whom. Laughing, she made him feel bad and it was his fault, he didn't know how to talk of anything else. From one evening to the next he couldn't tell what she was thinking, what she was going to say, and he withdrew into himself so as not to provide her with the chance of a sharp-tongued reply. She held him, she was the stronger; he needed her more than she needed him.

His thumb and forefinger gripped the page, searching for comfort in the awkwardly written numbers and words. Down the centre of each page was a line: on the right, the señorita's, on the left his. Balancing, exactly equal. Whatever she thought, however often she came down to look, here was the proof. He had never cheated her, not even a kilo, there was satisfaction in that.

Here were the figures for the first calf raised five years ago. The trouble she made before she agreed. 'And if it dies?' she asked.

'We both lose, señorita, for I shall have paid half.'

She looked at him suspiciously. 'No, you continue like your father, he was a good worker.'

A year later, asking again, she agreed, as long as her half of the costs was paid only when the animal was sold. Now if it died … He hesitated, cursed, mumbled agreement. A trap.

The ridicule if people found out. He told no one, not even Ana. Lacking the money to buy the calf on his own, he went to the bank. Within seven months, there it was written down: he'd paid off the loan and opened a savings account with his half of the profit. He smiled, mother never knew and thank God for that: she reproached him with nothing and yet a glance, a word from her could strike through him as though he were a child. She had nothing to thank the señorita for and wouldn't have spared him if she'd found out; she muttered under her breath each time the señorita appeared on her donkey to see what had been stolen.

Once, long before he died, his father said, 'That's how she is, the señorita.' And he, Miguel, understood: the inevitability of her nature stood before him like nature itself, even more determinedly invincible. She had her rights, she owned the land and complaining about her was a waste of time, even when over his mother's protests she exceeded those rights and searched the house for missing wheat.

He looked at the sky drained of colour, then at the water. His eye followed the irrigation furrows; it would just be enough. And next time? Six weeks. Less if this heat kept up. The shout echoed down, his irrigating time was at an end; with a swing of the hoe he turned the water into the main channel to the farmstead below. He breathed in deeply. He'd tell Juana tomorrow evening he was making an offer for Tío Bigote's land. But no, better to wait until the old man replied to the offer. Seven thousand, would it be enough? Across the watercourse on Madueño's land he noticed the pink shirt of the foreigner who'd bought the farm. El Inglés. The people said another one had come ... Yes, Tío Bigote's farm, there weren't many as good, it was better than Madueño's land. Tomorrow evening after work ...

37

Anxiety redoubled

'It won't last out,' Pepe said over his shoulder. 'I only irrigated four terraces last time.'

'Ugh!' he grunted, walking slowly behind.

Pepe stopped. 'The tomatoes worrying you? Hombre, there's no good worrying. The village borehole's always been unreliable …' He looked at his friend, expecting a good-natured laugh at the folly of worrying when there was nothing man or God could do about it.

'Yes.' Miguel stared at Pepe and the space between them lost its density and in the void he saw himself and Juana, separate. She would go and he couldn't stop her … Distantly, he saw Pepe pointing at terraces, at wheat that wasn't graining. He wasn't man enough to tell her she had to stay.

'What's the matter? Still thinking about those tomatoes?'

In the vacant space hope crystallized unexpectedly. 'Unless they strike water in the new borehole.'

Pepe laughed. The señorita would make sure they didn't start work on it again until the mayor had hit water; and with the señorita not paying her share there wouldn't be money enough to finish it anyway. 'Did you speak to her?'

Miguel shook his head. There was nothing one could do

about her. He wiped his forehead. Could he tell Pepe? No. What was there to keep her?

She was smiling, he tightened his grip on her arm, other couples moved slowly, watchfully in the evening *paseo*. Her cousin had got her a job in a foreigner's house on the coast. 'It's a good job, one hundred *duros* a month ...' The square slid away, forming a mist, and the houses, the people, the dry fountain floated in it, unreal to the core; and he foundered in the awareness that there was nothing to do but accept, because he had no weight in others' decisions, as impotent still as the child standing in the same square.

'She says she's going to find work on the coast,' he blurted out. 'I don't like it.'

Pepe stopped. So that was the trouble! Of course he wouldn't have worried about the crop. But Juana, yes.

'She's always talking about wanting to leave the village, saying that we should go to the town. To do what, I ask.'

'Yes, to do what? No, hombre, don't let her get ideas. That's what a woman wants: to command.'

'I know. I'll tell her she can't.' Tell her he was going to buy Tío Bigote's farm, tell her this was their village. A week before, as he'd promised himself, he'd been to see the old man.

'It'll have to be more than that,' Tío Bigote said quietly. 'Talk to Antonio Ríos, he can act for me,' and this answer, which he only half-dared expect, had set him afire with hope. The old man hadn't laughed at his presumption, hadn't sent him away; by the red-washed cottage the sharp old eyes had scrutinized and found him sufficient. And he, like an inheriting son, thought of the improvements he was going to make.

'A man who can't keep his woman in line is no man at all.' Pepe paused; in this alone Miguel, such a man for the rest, was different from others. 'But you've got to know how to deal with a woman, it's no good telling her "no" straight out, you see. I mean, come round to it a bit easy but then be firm.'

'You know I don't know how to talk.'

Pepe saw the pain on his face. 'Ah, don't be a fool, Miguel, you got her for a *novia*, didn't you?' His friend's hesitancy irritated him. He didn't want to lose his respect for Miguel, the best farmer he knew, because of a woman. 'Listen, you remember Manolo from Calahonda, he let his *novia* go down to the coast and she had an affair with a taxi-driver, didn't she? And what did he do when he found out? Went down there and stabbed her and strung himself up in a tree, poor devil. It's no good letting Juana go down there, I tell you. Isn't the pueblo good enough for her?'

'I don't know, I don't know what it is.' He wiped the sweat from his face. Manolo from Calahonda – yes, he could say, I don't want what happened to Manolo from Calahonda and his *novia*, eh? And laugh, make it a joke so she'd understand. Because if he told her now he was going to buy the farm she'd have even less reason for staying. Yes, that's all he could do.

But there was no word from Antonio Ríos. 'Nine thousand, he won't take less when he's asking eleven,' Antonio had said. 'Look at the land, Miguel, five good *fanegas*, not rock and goat pasture like Madueño's, which the Englishman bought. Twenty thousand he paid ...' and Miguel's hand, reaching for the notebook, had dropped.

'But I'm not a foreigner ...'

'The world's changing, Miguel.' Ríos squinted at him. 'Land that wasn't worth a peseta yesterday is worth ten today.'

Could he mortgage his share of the tomato crop? Even so he'd be short. And if the water failed ...

Pepe's voice cut through his thoughts. 'Look, they're fetching stone down to Madueño's land. What's the foreigner going to do – build himself a villa?'

'I don't know.' The piles of stone shone white on the far side of the watercourse; from El Mayorazgo he'd seen the mule trains bringing them down.

'They say there's another foreigner come, living in the sacristan's house.'

'Yes.'

'Have you see him?'

'Yes, a blond, he's been down.'

'Looking for land? If enough foreigners come they'll buy up the lot, eh? Not that your señorita will sell, she'll hang on and try to smuggle it to heaven, if they'll have her there.'

Miguel didn't reply. Behind his back the voices gathered strength, humiliation deepened. Not man enough, eh? Couldn't keep his betrothed where she belonged. The unseen faces smirked the loss of himself in the people's eyes through the loss of her. The pain was a warning, a summons to act.

38

Anxiety unassuaged

Leaving Pepe in the square, he went away to Antonio Ríos's house. Standing in the door, the middleman appeared to be waiting for him. 'Eight,' said Miguel, 'six on signing, the rest after the crop. That's my offer.'

'I'll talk to Tío Bigote, but I don't hold out much hope. Eight to eleven is a big gap. Now if we were talking of nine ...'

'Eight,' Miguel repeated. 'He knows who I am. If it were a foreigner that would be a different matter maybe.'

As though delivered of a burden, the sense of decision carried him down the street to Juana's. But he didn't tell her as they circled slowly in the evening *paseo*. For it was her decision that he was called on to respond to. She was going next week, she'd made up her mind.

A wordless plea rose in his throat. Juana, don't, I want you to stay ... Instead, the words that came out stopped her slow pacing, and she stared at him while the people in the endless chain eddied around them.

'Manolo of Calahonda! Ah, don't be stupid,' she replied coldly. 'You're not going to frighten me. Or perhaps you don't trust me, eh?'

No, no, he protested, sensing the danger, it wasn't her but the people's gossip.

'Don't worry about them, it's a good job and I'll be able to save. Isn't that what you want?'

Again an entreaty formed soundlessly on his lips. But she wouldn't heed him, he knew. Then refuse her the right to go, as Pepe said – and hear her refuse the refusal? No. He was frightened of losing her for good, his self-validation. Her arm lightly held in his, she was smiling in the distance. 'I'll be able to save.'

Save? 'Yes, save.' Sadness was closing in and she was trying to shake him free. 'You don't spend a peseta if you can borrow one.' Laughing feebly, threatened, he saw an escape open up, the possibility of accepting the impossibility of her going. They'd need the money. Yes. He started to tell her about the offer he'd made, and things returned to their place, the square grew familiar again; while she, only half listening, giggled about something with a girlfriend.

'So, of course, if you save ...' Yes, here was a reason, a justification to cling to until Pepe's exclamation on the way down.

'You mean she's going, you let her go? Because of the money? Well, if El Mayorazgo can't produce enough for one more then we're all lost.' And he knew it was true, the excuse would convince no one, not even when they knew he was buying the farm.

'Pepe, I told her about Manolo of Calahonda.'

'But Miguel!' What was the matter with him? Couldn't he talk to her like a man?

'It's my fault. I couldn't keep her, Pepe. I'm lost.'

'Don't be stupid. If that's how she is it's not your fault.'

'It's my fault because that's how I am.'

39

A real loss, a partial loss

Two days later she was gone, and the pain swelled and burst in his guts. Nothing existed but awareness of suffering, the part of him torn – gone, unimaginably absent in a foreigner's house. The pain propelled him into wanting to walk down immediately to fetch her back. But it was too late, he hadn't done what he should while there was still time. For five hundred pesetas a month he'd let her go.

Self-recrimination surged through him; he thumped the hoe into the dry earth, feeling Culebra's eyes fixed on him. The mask, so well contrived to hide insufficiency, clamped on his face. Spreading like a virus, the pain lay hidden under the skin.

'And how will the foreigner get the water down to the dam?' The old man's hooded eyes glanced at Miguel. 'If they strike water in the new borehole, that is.'

Leaning on his hoe, he stared at Culebra in the olive's shade: so this was what he had been driving at all along. His pain had blinded him to the words.

'The señorita doesn't like it,' the old man hissed as the echo of an explosion in the watercourse rumbled through the hills.

That was it, Culebra must have got it straight from her, they were as close as two fingers. There'd be no water, the tomatoes were lost. 'We won't irrigate then,' and the look of puzzled exclamation fixed on Miguel's face, a screen for his disillusionment.

'No one is going to make the foreigner a present of a channel across their land, are they?' Culebra grinned, showing three teeth.

'It's her own land,' he mumbled, 'it's as dry as August.'

'That's right, Miguelito, it's hers. They should never have allowed the foreigner to take over her share of the borehole. That was the mistake.'

'Since she wouldn't pay for the drilling to continue ...'

'Ah, you know her, she'd have paid once she saw there was going to be water. Then there'd have been no trouble about the channel. But now ... The trouble is that dam the foreigner's building, that's the trouble, I tell you.'

Culebra squatted, looking at the tomatoes. A good farmer, a likeable lad, getting a bit above himself though. A pity. You couldn't go against your landlord, he'd have to learn the way his father had learnt. 'How many plants have you got there?'

'A thousand. So we won't be able to irrigate?'

'No. We'll have to hold out.' He'd made so much from last year's early crop, the old man thought enviously, that it had put ideas in his head.

Miguel's fingers felt the tops of the vines. They'd last another couple of weeks without irrigation, no more. Five thousand *duros* hanging on the fate of these vines. Was the señorita prepared to lose her half share? He pushed his hat back to wipe his forehead. Yes, she must be willing to lose two and a half thousand to make sure he didn't earn them. She must know his plans and was wanting to punish him. Antonio Ríos hadn't replied. And all the while the *novia* was in some stranger's house.

'Yes,' came Culebra's voice, 'it's the dam that's the trouble. The foreigners are all right as long as they don't mix in things they don't know.'

Miguel took the hoe to the next row of vines. There was relief in the force of the arms, in the shoulders bearing down on the earth. The clods broken up by the hoe, the soil turned friable, protecting the moisture from the sun's metallic heat, which beat on his neck and shoulders, on his arms as he turned the earth.

'And if the dam doesn't hold? There was a dam burst somewhere once when I was young, about your age I was, and …' Culebra's voice circled slowly round the memory of disaster.

'There's no danger as long as there's no water.' The edge in his words was softened by a respectful glance at Culebra.

'Ah, it'll fill in winter, that'll be when the danger comes. That wall he's building, *hijo*, it isn't strong. If it breaks, the water will sweep everything away.'

'Yes?' If the wall broke, yes, perhaps Culebra was right. Up high like that, the water would sweep over the farms. Casa Colorada. The dam was the root of the trouble, whatever the blond said, if it weren't for the dam the señorita … He lost the thought, seemed outside, straining to catch it as he bent over the furrow.

'That foreigner, the blond, comes down here a lot.'

Miguel nodded.

'Even before they started the dam, I used to see him down at Casa Colorada. Must be looking for land, eh?'

Uprooted, the vine toppled over the mis-struck hoe as he stared at the old man.

'They've got money, the foreigners. Tío Bigote will be wanting to sell, he's getting on, and with no sons to help.'

'Yes?' The blood pounded in his head. Brothers-in-law, Culebra would know.

'Well, that's what I've heard. The blond's interested in it. Antonio Ríos is the middleman.'

Miguel stood looking at him. For a moment everything fell into place – the blond, Casa Colorada, the dam – then shattered.

Culebra stirred, his eyes betraying nothing. To make sure, he spoke again. There was no answer. That's it, he thought, the señorita was right. Ech! The foreigners putting ideas in the people's heads. Miguelito should have known, the señorita had been good to him. Ay! Cheating her. He flung a stone at the goats, looking at Miguel who hadn't moved, hadn't noticed his going, who stood transfixed among the dry plants in the afternoon sun.

40

Sadness and guilt

Ana found him bent over the earth. Groping, he watched the fingers slipping on the plant's stem as though unrelated to him, detached from any purpose but that of pretence. She mustn't know. What a fool! To be deluded by false hopes. The lash of reproach struck beyond him somewhere, sadness protected him from guilt, nothing stirred. Through the lassitude he heard Ana's voice saying the grass was burnt dry, he'd have to find fodder for the calf. He stayed stooped over the furrow.

'Miguel, there's hardly anything left for the calf. What's the matter? What's wrong with you?'

'Nothing,' he mumbled.

'You've never been like this. You haven't been eating, you woke me last night with your dreaming. What is it?'

He shrugged, resenting her concern, the implication in her voice that she knew the reason, had heard the rumours. What did she want with him? She who had slaved so he could put money in the bank for this, for nothing – she could have been betrothed by now if he hadn't kept her down here herding cattle. She knew it, he knew it, she'd said it. He didn't want her concern.

'It's the girl, isn't it? Ever since she went down to the coast.' His passive, stooped back angered her. She wouldn't allow him to suffer like this. 'It's her fault, Miguelito, only you won't admit it, you're too kind-hearted.'

'Go in, woman, go in.' What did she know? Kind-hearted. There had been whispers meant to be overheard – flaunting her new-found foreigner's ways, when she came back for the first time two Sundays ago.

'I'll ride if I want to, Miguel. If it pleases me ...'

'Pleases! No! People are talking.'

'People? They're always talking, Miguel.'

'I forbid you, Juana, I forbid, do you hear?' She shrugged, turning away to laugh with someone, and rage deflated like a child's balloon. He was right and yet she made him look a fool, ignoring him, refusing to mention his outburst, probably disobeying him at this very moment ...

'Go in, woman, I say,' he cried, twisting his hand round the stem of the plant, guilt lashing out to annihilate her.

Ana started to go, overcame the impulse to obey. 'She's bad for you, Miguel, she's making you ill, I can feel it, I know. That's the sort she is, ever since she left you've been ...'

'Leave me, leave me alone,' he cried. She, too, why was she torturing him? The anguish in his voice frightened her. 'Miguelito, come in out of the heat.'

These past months there had been flashes of irritation she had never seen before. Only the other day he'd put her to shame about having her hair done – and in front of the foreigner. Picking on her, rejecting her – she felt the danger of losing him; he could never share himself out between them and Juana, she thought.

'When the furrow's finished,' he grunted. Why do this to her, it's not her fault ... The guilt turned on itself, burnt into him. He shouldn't have tried, it was beyond him, dangerous to reach out to make real a hope. His life had never been his to make. Without speaking, without looking at him, his father had taken the army volunteer's paper and torn it up. Watching the pieces fall on the floor, the fissure opened, splitting him from reality: he should have known he would fail.

'Son,' his mother wailed, 'what are you thinking of? The army! Leaving us, is that how a son acts?'

'There's nothing to stay here for,' he shouted, guilt bursting into anger. Obeying, always obeying. For months thereafter apathy kept him shut in himself, he seemed not to exist outside the effort of going each night to look for a job to carry him through the next day, outside the flashes of self-reproach for his lack of will. A heaviness overcame him, sadness invaded him, there was nothing left.

The taste of those days returned. He looked at Ana walking towards the cottage. Betraying her and his mother to make a bond with another, betraying those who needed him, who had no one else. But no! Juana was to be part of them, not he part of her ... Ech! They didn't want her, she didn't want them, there wasn't enough to satisfy them all. Pepe or Antonio would know how to impose his will on a woman the way a man should, but ... No, there was nothing to bring her back. Not now.

Sadness flowed slowly through him, the strength of his arms became a weariness. The illusion evaporated, draining in whorls like the heat from the land. Casa Colorada would never be his. It was a dream guilty of having been dreamt, a dream of sufficiency, of outgrowing dependency. A dream giving the strength to dominate discord, unite mother, sister and wife in the proof of his worth. It was to have been his and there, by those red walls, they, too, were to have been his.

He stared over the terraces. The heat-cracked land was impermeable to thought that would attach it to him. The line that had oriented the land in a perspective of aims, like a furrow determining the water's flow, had been cut, and there was no future in which to see himself. The world had narrowed to him alone.

41

Sadness and anger

The sound of sliding shale made him stoop over the wheat, the sickle glinting between the thin stalks. The dogs started to bark, churning dust as they rushed across the terrace. No, he wouldn't give him the satisfaction of seeing his defeat. How stupid he'd been! Of course a foreigner didn't walk for the love of it, didn't ask questions as though just to chat, didn't talk about water unless he had an interest in land. The blond had fooled him. Only a few weeks ago, standing there looking surprised, he'd pretended he didn't know Tío Bigote or the farm. He'd deceived him deliberately, more dishonest for all his apparent concern than the señorita who said nothing, gave nothing and with whom he knew where he stood ... Ech! It was all over, the mistake was to think there'd ever been a chance; the tomatoes could ripen or die, it made no difference. Foreigners had money and with money a man could do as he liked.

He tried to feel himself reaping, tried to let the hand control the cut, but as always there was a void now through which he looked: the hand grasped the stalks, the left leg moved, the sickle swung – the movements were made but he was outside them. A wave of sadness suffused him, as purposeless as the movements he watched himself make. When the waves came he let the sickle fall and stood blindly while the sadness absorbed him. Towards the end, his father had stood staring like that, leaning on the hoe, his eyes empty of hope, and Miguel had imagined the effects of age, the tiredness that did not vanish with a night's sleep when he tossed and moaned as though, in place of the words he never spoke, his body were protesting at the weight of the plough, the heaviness of the earth. A father who stared accusingly, mutely at him in his dreams from which he awoke in a sweat. Why not be content with things as they were, one year after another, like him? Why the wanting, the reaching beyond himself, the thinking he could better his lot? For what? For nothing. Dreams that the foreigner had smashed.

'Hola!' A nerve of defence was all that remained. The foreigner stopped a few steps away. He never came right up to you, never, always kept his distance: watchful and calculating – the inexplicable hesitancy that used to be good for a smile now explained. A flash of hatred struck out at him and was repressed before attaining its object: behind the dark glasses the red, sweat-streaked face showed nothing, as usual. A viscous presence that had deceitfully congealed. What did he want? He waited for the blond who moved, not closer but into the shade of the carob, to speak. They were punishing him for aiming too high.

As though from a distance he heard the accented voice: the blond had just come from the dam, the retaining wall was almost half built. The note of congratulatory excitement was there as usual, as though the blond expected him to share in an extraordinary gift. The deception brought another surge of hatred which he disguised in sullenness. 'Ah, they're still working then?'

'Of course! Bob has already got two miners working on the new borehole. With a bit of luck the dam will still fill this summer. You and all the other farmers round here will have plenty of water. One hundred million litres, Miguel!'

He thought, the blond, that only a foreigner could imagine a reservoir. Only a foreigner would be that clever! Ech! 'My brother had that idea. During the war: a reservoir for the collective. But there wasn't time ...' He bent down and picked up a stone, which he sent whirling across the terrace to fall with a crash in the corn. Would the blond understand? No! Because he answered that *this* dam was real.

'You've seen it, the retaining wall they're building. It won't be long before it's finished.'

He picked up the hook and began reaping again, his back to the foreigner. The wheat had little grain. From high on the slope came the sound of cow-bells; Ana was bringing the cattle down. He hadn't thought of his brother for a long time, and the memory brought with it a painful awareness: Antonio wouldn't have allowed himself to be taken in by a foreigner; he'd have struck a deal with Tío Bigote long ago, got the farmers together to continue drilling the new borehole without waiting on anyone; he'd have found a way to get water down to the farmsteads ... But he wasn't Antonio, could never emulate him. From forgotten depths, a child's rage welled up and spilled over into his nerves: encompassed his brother and the blond and turned back on himself: he wasn't worthy of his brother, had only himself to blame ...

'Ah, it's time already.' He dropped the sickle and walked towards the house, past the terrace of tomatoes where the canes threw long shadows in the sun that was setting in a blaze of bronze. The duty to act, to decide what to do, agitated a nerve that shuddered, then fell immobilizingly slack. He must, but he couldn't. Inertia closed in, barring awareness that the impossibility of acting was an impossibility of wanting to act. He couldn't – no, in reality he couldn't want: in the loss of his goal the purpose of action was lost, and all that remained was a sense of emptiness.

Behind him he heard the blond say, 'The tomatoes are drying up.' Suddenly the continuing reminder of his loss penetrated the emptiness; he felt himself stopping, turning, heard his own voice:

'You have to give too, you can't only take.' He saw the foreigner stop and his mouth drop, felt the anguish that came on his face, turned and walked on, the sense of aggression already being replaced by a feeling of guilt. The blond didn't follow. By the low door Ana was waiting.

'Miguelito, there's hardly any fodder left. What are you going to do?' He didn't reply. 'Miguelito,' she whined, 'you've got to do something. Tell the señorita …' He remained staring at the tiles.

'There's nothing to be done,' he said at last.

The phrase struck through her as it was intended to. 'But how can you say that?' she cried. 'Do you want to bring us to ruin?'

Through the trees the foreigner's white shirt was approaching. Hadn't she understood yet? 'It'd be better to finish once and for all.'

'Miguel!' Horror-stricken, her eyes fixed on him. Words substituting for action, the phrase ballooned outside him, empty of meaning, coming from nowhere. He watched it bewildered, seeking its source. Then she laughed. 'Ah, brother, how you tease sometimes!'

'I said: it would be better to finish once and for all.'

She opened her mouth but nothing came out. His eyes were fixed on the tiles at his feet. The silence was unbroken, then as the foreigner turned the corner, she spoke. 'Pepe sent a message, the *novia* is coming to the village on Saturday. She told Salvarito in Torre del Mar.'

'Ah!' He didn't move. The blond's shadow passed in front of him, stopping by the door close to Ana, the voice shrilling out anxiously, 'The dam will mean forty or more hours of water for El Mayorazgo.'

Saturday! Ah! Suddenly hate flared. Impregnable, unbending, Juana stood before him, her voice taunting: 'If it pleases me to cut my hair ...'

No! He'd looked at her that Sunday and hadn't believed his eyes. Flaunting her short hair without shame, like a foreign woman. People were talking, someone in the village had seen her in the foreigner's garden wearing trousers like a man. He no longer pleaded, he ordered her; she wouldn't obey. Humiliated, he lashed out, willing her destruction without wishing the means. He feared the revenge his rage would unleash.

Ana saw his jaw muscles clench. 'That much water!' she cried, clutching at the straw to bring him back to them. Attracted by the sound of the foreigner's voice, their mother appeared in the doorway. The blond went on explaining, his words barely comprehensible in his anxiety to make himself understood.

'There's barely any fodder left, the calf will have to be sold,' Ana said.

'No fodder!' screeched the old woman. 'Ay! Ay!'

The hatred turned on itself. Aggression brought guilt, guilt self-recognition: a hope momentarily stirred. The strength of submission, of humbled expiation, of being himself.

'The calf will fetch a better price in Torre del Mar where the foreigners buy,' exclaimed the blond.

Worthlessness making an offering of worth, humbly, openly paying tribute, conquering by admitting defeat.

'Yes, yes,' Ana agreed. Avoid the middlemen in the village, sell direct. 'Yes, Miguel, that's what must be done.' Never before had she dared offer advice.

The last hope: a present, an offering of such cost that gratitude would overwhelm her, something from him to which she could point, an unbreakable bond. On condition she returned to the village.

'Miguel! That's what must be done.'

'Eh?' In the void the ornate idea shone like a pinpoint of light. Dimly he became aware of their faces, and the light failed to hold off the reality into which their eyes plunged him. Fodder, water ... A surge of sadness engulfed him. Giving, taking. 'Ana, those apricots ...' He watched her go. Enclosed in the sadness his mother stood at a distance looking at him. Her love misplaced. He would show her now. 'There won't be water, they say, the señorita is against.'

What did he mean, the blond asked. He told them. 'Your friend shouldn't have taken the señorita's share of the borehole.'

'Son, didn't I tell you?' he heard his mother cry. 'The mistress wouldn't give you a needle to take a thorn from your hand. Didn't I tell you?'

His head remained bowed to accept her blame.

'We'll see about that,' the blond said.

'Yes?' He grimaced. Talk, foreigner, talk as much as you like, the señorita will always have the last word.

Ana returned with the basket.

'How much do I owe?'

He looked up at the foreigner standing there with his hand in his pocket waiting to bring out the money. For a moment scorn burnt through the sadness, inflected his voice.

'Hombre, what nonsense!'

Looking flustered the blond repeated his thanks. 'Let's go up to the new borehole when you've got time. You'll get water, I'm sure of that.'

'If God wills.' No one else, no one else and what can He care about the emptiness? And he waited head bowed for his mother to speak.

42

Remission

Madre! Expelled from emptiness, the sigh was lost in the empty land. Madre! A longing for stillness, absolute peace. The hook fell and his hand brushed the pocket where the bracelet lay wrapped. Over him the sun pressed its molten weight, around him the land burnt in its glare, but the heat was not part of the emptiness in which the longing arose to extinguish the fragments obsessively pulsing in front of his eyes: her smile: the bracelet replaced in the paralysed hand: the hand still outstretched in a frozen grip: 'No, Miguel, no …' Distraught fragments, ineludible images: the hand stretched out in failure for eternity, the irrevocable words that severed the last link. It was all over, there was nothing, never had been. What a fool to have thought there could be!

A folly which, while he'd awaited her return that Saturday, had lifted him in hope like a twig buoyed by the water's flow that coursed once more down a furrow to the future. Which had given him the strength to go with the blond to see the new borehole, joyfully feeling in his pocket, as he walked up the track, the weight of the talismanic gold bracelet against his leg. He had kept it on him day and night since going to Torre del Mar, caressing the smooth metal in his hands, gazing at it as though in its circumference the future were inscribed. It would overwhelm her, a bracelet such as no one else owned, to be shown off without shame, Tío Bigote's farm to wear on her wrist! Yes. All his savings! He'd spent it all to prove that her life belonged to him and the village. Let the blond buy the land.

As they came over the hill and the dam came into view below, he stopped. Culebra's fearful predictions returned. 'Will it hold?'

'Of course,' the blond replied. His friend Bob was experienced in matters like this. The tone of voice was scornful, trying to make his fears seem foolish. The presentiment brought a shiver.

'Ah yes, if not we'll all end up in the sea,' he attempted to joke.

The blond laughed; and it was then that he knew that this same voice could more easily annihilate hope than fear. He walked on. A few paces ahead he muttered in a tone he hoped and feared the blond would hear:

'The foreigners bring work but they take our land.'

The blond said nothing. In silence they walked on. Hadn't he heard or did he choose to ignore the words? Would he still deny the truth? Ech! It no longer mattered. His fingers stroked the gold in his pocket, caressing his possession of her, her oneness with him, the life's propitiatory offering he was wagering on a future together. Nothing else was of importance now ...

Madre! Memories haunted by failure, doomed from the start.

'Miguel!' Ana's shadow fell on the wheat; in the echoing vault the hand was stretched out. 'Miguel, when are you going to sell the calf? It's a month now ...'

Alone with her, his silence must break. He looked unseeingly at her. Juana's closeness in place of theirs. In trying he had destroyed the closeness within: mother and Ana had been betrayed, to be true to her was to be false to them, false to himself who was bound to them; in breaking this he had broken with them, shattered the closeness and was rightly condemned.

She laid a hand on his arm but it touched nothing in him. 'Miguel,' she repeated, 'Miguel, it's me.' In the silence her eyes implored him to speak. Gift of repentance and promise, substitute for the land, moment of hope paid for in despair, the bracelet lay meaningless in his hand. Rejecting it, she rejected him, the self that was true: the yielding creature who tried to melt into her, to suck tenderness from a gratifying breast. Madre! Unworthy of such tenderness as only a woman, a mother, could give.

She heard the sigh, thought she knew the cause, unaware of the bracelet that lay in his pocket. 'Mother was worried, don't take it to heart.' He stared, silent, her words falling like stones. 'Miguel, mother didn't mean it,' she cried, trying to get through the blankness to something alive, unaware that the silence hid only hollowness inside. Yet she, not their mother, had seen his bowed face, seen him whiten and cringe as she had cried out their dependence on him, his obligation to them, as though for the sake of another he was forsaking them; had felt their mother trying to pull him back, restore the common bond that since their father's death they had tacitly shared. Meaning only to warn him, had she unthinkingly destroyed the bond a mother's tenderness had forged? A tender dependency the more pervasively dominant the more patent the domination of the father's world; a sweet necessity with its roots deep in the past the father's death had served to strengthen; a source of submission he had tried to escape by seeking it in another without destroying its source …

Seeing into the emptiness, the women had judged: bowed before mother, *novia*, señorita, he accepted the ineluctable guilt, the recriminations, the confirmation of solitude into which a hand stretched uselessly to offer itself.

Ana's hand dropped. Despairingly she wondered what ought to be done, rejecting the idea, as she walked away, of telling Pepe: the family web, just the three of them, had borne the world too long to be broken now by the admission that something was happening they couldn't sustain. She looked back at him as the church bells started to peal, saw him standing there motionless and began to run. 'Water!' she cried. 'They've hit water, Miguel.'

In the silence the bells pealed distantly in him, confirming what had been done that self-recrimination could no longer elude.

'Miguel! Miguel!' Her arm was pulling him. 'Don't you hear?'

Yes, beneath the peals he heard the single, slow toll of absolute peace, passivity reunited beyond strife with itself, the sole means of evading the inescapable truth. He allowed her to lead him blindly across the terrace: to finish once and for all, there was nothing else. Certainty illuminated the void with a distant light; a pinpoint of certitude that deepened the emptiness. The light was a goal he could not yet reach; inhibition protected him from the power to act, from realizing the way to escape. Rounding the corner, they stopped, overwhelmed. The light pulsed violently against his eyes and he seemed, without moving, to stretch out to her, to run towards Juana who sat under the vine. Through the haze he saw her smiling at him, waiting for him. He swayed; forgiven, she had come back for him. Shaking off Ana's hand, he moved towards her and —

43

Dolores burst through the granary door crying, 'They're coming, they're coming, señor!' Her face was alight with excitement, in strange contradiction to the feelings she had expressed over the past weeks concerning the event. But now that the civil governor and his cortege had actually arrived she seemed overwhelmed.

Looking down the street from his bedroom window, John saw the officials in their falangist white jackets and blue shirts getting out of big black cars which, with their motorcycle escort, filled the square. The new mayor, similarly attired, and other village dignitaries had gathered to meet them. Villagers gawked at this unaccustomed display, whose pretext was the inauguration of Benalamar's first public lighting. Massive angled steel brackets, painted silver and carrying lamps large enough to illuminate a city street, had been bolted to the facades of houses in the square which, on the mayor's express orders, had all been newly whitewashed. Pots of flowers hung from the walls as the result of another municipal ordinance. And, it was rumoured, the streets and square were to be concreted over shortly.

The new mayor was a forward-looking man, Bob said. Though he shared some of Bob's convictions about Benalamar's possibilities, the village coffers were as empty as under his predecessor. To pay for his 'modernization' plan he had slapped new taxes on houses and on fish sold in the village, and taken a number of people off the municipal poor list. It was these arbitrary measures that brought adverse comments from Dolores, who more than once claimed that the village was better off under the old mayor. Moreover, she saw the reduction of the poor list as a mayoral swindle because the newly 'non-poor' would now have to pay for their medical prescriptions. 'As far as I know,' she said derisively, 'there's only one chemist here, and he and the doctor are as thick as two thieves. And who is the chemist? Well, he just happens to be the new mayor!'

John had paid little attention to these changes or to Dolores's comments. But the sight of the crowd in the street induced him to leave his house for the first time in a number of days. He made for the bar, which was deserted except for a man leaning against the counter. John recognized Manolo, Miguel's cousin, the miner, whom he hadn't seen since they'd struck water, and greeted him warmly. 'Not going out there to watch the show?'

'Na! Not with that bunch of rogues.' Manolo called for a beer and passed it to John. 'They live off our backs. The people here forget easily … You were friendly with my cousin, weren't you?'

'I didn't help him when he needed it.'

'Ah!' He appeared surprised. 'Well, I wasn't here. When I heard the news I didn't believe it. But I thought straight away, the señorita's to blame.'

'Yes? I'm not sure any one person's to blame. He wanted to buy Casa Colorada, did you know that? And to stop him someone put it about that I was going to buy it.'

'I heard, yes.'

'Well, it wasn't me.'

'Perhaps it was another foreigner. Look how the land is being sold on the coast.'

Another foreigner! Bob? No, it couldn't be, he hadn't the money.

'He needed that farm, Manolo, the same as he needed the *novia*.'

'The land, yes. There's no sharecropper who doesn't need his own land because the land should be for those who work it. But as long as these' – nodding at the square – 'keep things as they are it'll never happen.'

'And the *novia*!'

'She wasn't any good for him, she's without shame. Going to El Mayorazgo like that after what she'd already done. No, he didn't need her.' Manolo drank down his beer and John ordered another. 'Poor cousin, he went mad when the water came and threw himself in the watercourse.'

'His world shut in on him, projects that were vital to him were cut off.'

'If the señorita hadn't been out only for herself he could have had water. That's what I say.'

'No one here commits suicide for lack of water. Isn't that what everyone says? There must have been more reasons than that.'

'You mean, he lost the will to live?'

'Perhaps. No, because when the world shuts in, when there's no future left, one's cut off from acting and even suicide becomes an impossible act. It must be when the will to act returns because of some change that really changes nothing …'

Manolo stared at him uncomprehendingly. At that moment ranks of white jackets and blue shirts went past the windows and people shouted out, 'Viva Franco! Viva Franco!'

'Ech! The señorita made him go back on his word. A man's word. When she said fetch the calf back he obeyed. He had no fight in him, that was the trouble, and she knew it.'

'And the *novia*, didn't she know it too? Both these women.'

He paused to drink. 'The fact is, Miguel was too good for her, too good for them all. It's painful to think how he must have suffered to have done what he did.'

A flash of light, so strong that it almost burnt the eyes, lit up the cavernous bar and the square outside. Clapping broke out and more cheers for the Generalissimo. Men began to push into the bar. 'Eh, Manolo, what do you think of the lights?'

'It's the new age,' he laughed, 'we're all going to be modern now.' And then, with a sharp look at John before the men closed in, he added: 'You can change a *novia*, señor, but you can't change a landlord. That's why the señorita's to blame.'

In the street John saw Bob's figure looming over the crowd which was waiting for the cortege to leave. The motor-cycle outriders were already in position, the roar of their engines reverberating in the small square. In an instant the cars and their outriders were sweeping down the brightly lit street, bringing to an end a visit that had lasted half an hour at most.

Bob was walking towards him with Ignacio, the town hall secretary. For a moment the three of them stood exchanging pleasantries; then Bob begged Ignacio's permission to talk to John.

'Well, things are now really looking up,' Bob said when they were alone. 'My lawyers have been here and sorted things out, the mayor has been very cooperative. We were able to do him a little favour, you see.' The mayor had understood that the cost of taking water for the village from the new borehole would be too high. Bob had helped him get engineers up who had assured him there was plenty of water to be had from the old borehole if they dug another hundred metres into the mountainside. 'The mayor's well in with the civil governor, as you can see, and he's getting a special credit to do the work.'

'Was that the end of the legal case?' John asked, and Bob

nodded. 'That's good. The village'll have water and you can start work again on the dam.'

'Well, not immediately. It seemed best not to offend certain susceptibilities before they start deepening the village borehole. That was the agreement,' Bob replied.

'Ah-ha!'

'It'll only be a short time. In fact, I wanted to tell you I'm going to Tangier for a bit of a holiday. I'll be back, of course, before work on the dam starts again. But you know the way people here exaggerate – if I told them they'd probably think I was going for good. So if you hear anything said, perhaps you'd put people straight.'

There was a frankness that wasn't quite frank in his look. But John no longer cared. 'All right,' he said. 'Well, have a good time.'

'Thanks. Oh, by the way, if anything happens you can get me care of American Express. I'm leaving tonight.' He raised his hand in mock salute over the heads of the crowd.

John turned to go home. As he pushed open the street door he felt the first drops of rain, a thinner, more persistent rain than on the previous occasion. In the granary he heard it falling steadily on the tile roof and beginning to course over the gutter spout. By the time he went to bed it was dripping through the mud and cane ceiling at the far end of the granary.

In the morning rivulets were running down the village streets and pools of water lay on the granary floor. John got a bucket and Dolores saucepans, and the sound of Chinese torture began. At noon the rain lifted, only to resume an hour later with a violent thunderstorm that rumbled over the village and mountains for the rest of the afternoon and evening. The accompanying rain was torrential. By nightfall the streets were awash, a portion of the granary ceiling had fallen in, and it was still raining.

{222}

Dolores insisted that John move his work table into the bedroom. Reluctantly he agreed. It irritated him to have withstood the granary's heat and dim light for so long only to be driven out by rain. Rain! A month ago a downpour like this would have solved so many problems; now, it seemed to him little more than an annoying distraction. Outside, as he wrote, he could hear the rain beating against the shutters.

44

Remission negated

And then, as Miguel turned for the third night from Juana's closed door, the idea suddenly locked, and in the cold lucid light that flooded the void the fragments of despair were fused and surpassed in a movement beyond the exclusions towards the inescapable choice, to transcend destruction by destroying himself. Without hesitation and without other recourse, he moved, unaware of the eyes but aware of their truth, hearing the certainty without hearing the words, down the street to the shop and then on through the square to the top of the track …

To follow his steps to the end is too painful now; but he cannot be left a victim of fate, as though his choice were explained by the force of events, by lack of some will to continue to live. One has to believe that his act was not a meaningless consequence of repudiation, exclusion and loss but a way of assuming and overcoming these.

Juana's impossible visit, a miracle that nothing could have led him to expect, was taken as a sign of redeemed possibility, a tender equivalent of the humility and forgiveness the bracelet had been intended to mean. And although he couldn't speak, the walls of the narrowing void must have been breached as he reached out to her within this new space that joined and yet kept them apart still. Possibility: she was there; but possibility, too, as what isn't yet – a lack to be filled, a goal to reach. Long after she'd gone this goal crystallized.

It was most probably then that he spoke to Ana, not about Juana, but about the farm. A fear haunted his speaking of her lest Ana, suspicious of this unsanctioned visit, cast doubt on the miraculous hope whose foundation was faith, not contentious fact. For a miracle is faith in the impossible. And Ana, as joyful to hear him speak as she was confused, was more joyful still and still further confused by the plan that was being revealed.

'Ay Miguel! What are you saying? That you're going to free us?'

'No, sister, no.' No sooner had he raised her hopes than he shattered them with unverified doubts.

'But perhaps it isn't true. Ask Tío Bigote!'

Immediately inhibition clamped down, a prevention of action that defended the self from the anguished uncertainty of the results of his acts. To go to him now would be to expose insufficiency to self-sufficient strength. 'No, no,' he shook his head.

'Well, ask the blond then!'

She understood a man's reluctance to ask favours of equals, but the foreigner was nothing in this network of respect. He saw that; yet he hesitated, for while the blond could not exclude him as a man in the way of Tío Bigote or Pepe, a single word from him could still shatter hope. Moreover, the bracelet was still in his pocket: could he bring himself to return it? Would the jeweller in Torre del Mar pay him in full?

'Ask the blond! Ask him!' she insisted.

'No.' But something inside him said yes. Yet it was several days before he went up, for although a perspective had opened within it, the depression hadn't vanished. Moments of anguish and inhibition, moments of self-reproach and destruction persisted despite – or rather because of – the new-found possibility of acting. Before he could go he had to find some innocuous excuse; over the following days it must have come to him that, if there was no work on the land, he could earn a labourer's day-wage on the dam. The figures revolved in his head, were entered mentally in the notebook where their solidity brought assurance that he, so unsure of the validity of his existence, existed indisputably.

He came up to ask first for work, then to ask about the farm. But immediately he entered the granary he knew his mistake, saw it in the irritated look, heard it in the cold, distant voice. The blond sat hunched over a stack of paper in the darkened room, and Miguel was taken aback, felt confidence drain away. Standing dazed, by the door, he stammered an excuse. The blond got up slowly and offered him a chair; he shook his head. In the thickening despair he heard the other's questions about the land, the calf.

'What! Haven't you sold it yet?' The foreigner's voice cut through to the guilty emptiness within, revealing its indifference to even that guilt in its cold invulnerability.

'Tomorrow, yes, I'll ...' In his own voice he heard the self-condemnation that was holding him back. Blankly he said: 'I've come to ask for work on the dam.'

The burst of sudden laughter, the blond's exclamation, seared confirmation across the screen of his mind, cauterizing the membrane of hope that held the void from closing in. 'Ah, I thought ...'

'The señorita will change her mind ... The water can't run to waste all summer,' the blond said determinedly.

'No.' Now his hatred swept over her as well, was repressed and turned on himself in recriminations intended for everyone who refused to recognize their blame for his plight. Had the instinct of anger not been repressed in fear of an annihilating retort from those who (like his father) were dominant over him, his retaliation would have been as swift and brusque as it was with Ana. Instead, the repression bred guilt for his failure to say what he felt, and the failure, proving his insufficiency, bred a yet deeper guilt.

'After all these months what's another week or two?'

He stared at the blond who contemptuously refused to recognize the limit he'd reached, twisted him because he knew there was nothing he could do. His mouth opened to speak but the words failed to come.

'What's the point of leaving the farmstead now? Be patient.'

'I can't ...' The wind's roar suppressed the words, the sheets of paper whirled through the air and beat at his face, fell at his feet. The foreigner was scrambling on his knees, his unintelligible world galvanized round the bits of paper which uncomprehendingly Miguel stooped to pick up. Exclusive, excluding, the foreigner's small, hermetic world closed in on him.

'Thank you ... My work,' the blond gasped, trying to order the papers.

His hand reached for the door as the blond backed round a circle of hope, even as he said he couldn't hold out hope. Ah! The last illusion was too dear to be shattered by this demeaning voice coming out of the dark, too precious still to be confirmed in its hopelessness. He opened the door and went down the stairs, the rejection confirmed, the void sealing him in.

Most probably it was Ana who took the next step. For her the blond's words would have little weight, must not be allowed to undermine her brother's tenuous improvement. The calf had to be sold. Tío Bigote might be able to buy it and at the same time ...

While the blond's repudiation had struck at his roots, the first of more decisive ones to come, he did not live it as the total loss of himself. Ana's determination could blind him still, and he allowed her to take him to see Tío Bigote.

The old man, one could guess (for no one has said what happened), was surprised to be offered the calf but too shrewd to refuse it; he had enough foodstuff stored to hold out through the drought and, moreover, he was able to knock down the price. Without the customary bargaining, without even a word, Miguel nodded agreement. Then Ana, seeing that he wouldn't speak, asked the old man herself and, his earth-worn face more than ever dissimulating surprise, he would have replied:

'Ah, now there's water and what with the dam, it will be worth a bit more for a foreigner to buy.'

Some phrase of the sort would have been enough. Hearing no more than was expected Miguel walked blindly away, leaving Ana alone and defenceless before the old man. She saw her mistake – and later her hatred of the foreigner was in part perhaps explicable as a projection of her self-hatred for what she had done – and ran after him. When she reached the farmstead she found he had gone.

45

Ultimate lucidity

Barely aware, he had set off up the track to the village. Miguel had not seen Juana since her visit to the farmstead, but he knew that this Friday evening she was due from the coast. Despair narrowed will to a single goal: to have proof of the miracle by her agreement to stay. In this narrowed vision, Tío Bigote and the blond existed as goads: his failure there could still be made good if proof of her constancy could be assured.

Bitter though it was, Casa Colorada's loss could be sustained without loss of esteem in others' eyes: no one could reproach him for not gaining what few could ever have as nearly attained, and for perhaps the first time he saw through a part of the falsehood he had created himself: a man's self-sufficiency, dignity and pride did not come from money or owning land, but persisted and were proved in a stony endurance, a rock-like observance of certain rights, among them a man's dominion over a woman. If Casa Colorada were to have been proof of himself in her eyes, the loss could be surpassed and survived if Juana were to prove his self-sufficiency in others' eyes.

In anguish he walked past her house, returned, walked past the closed door again. A surge of hope, shot through with fear, overcame him: on this moment was staked all that remained, and he lifted his hand to knock on the door.

We know what happened, we know her reasons. Miguel never knew, but the difference was small. Had she had the courage to tell him, would he have responded by laying the blame of inconstancy where it was deserved? It seems doubtful; in the event even this escape was denied by the unopened door, by the tangible exclusion that derided all hope. He stumbled away. If there had been hope it was because *he* had hoped; if there was none it was because *he* was nothing. Self-recrimination bore down remorselessly, was transformed obscurely into a logic of guilt: failure to act like a man merited a punishment to fit the nonbeing he was.

Tormented by his reasoning, he got up exhausted the next morning before the sun rose and walked without knowing where, obsessively impelled by the torture of thoughts that the movement was meant to resolve and evade.

Hearing the cows still in the stalls next to the room, Ana got up and looked for him. From the threshing floor, the countryside opened away and in that motionless expanse under the pale dawn sky she saw his hunched figure by the place where the water still poured uselessly down. She started to run and screamed as he fell, his arms outstretched in a futile embrace, seeing him splash like an animal trapped, getting to him as his face lifted for air and pulling at him with the strength of despair. He came out of the watercourse without resisting her, without saying a word, and all that day until evening she never let him out of her sight.

Would he have drowned if it had not been for her? Was this the punishment or was it a desperate appeal to be saved from the self-punishment he meant to inflict?

All that day the cold sensation of sinking, the dreaded water and then the escape, stirred an insensate flicker of self-exculpation and hope. That evening, hearing from Pepe that Juana had not been at her house the evening before, he returned to the village, and again was refused.

The impossibility now of eluding his loss and exclusion – his worthlessness made real in the barred door behind which she sat – gave a further dimension to the self-punishment he was about to inflict. In destroying himself he would destroy her in him, the accusing eyes would be stilled for ever and she, the permanent reflection of his guilt, would in turn become a permanent figure of guilt. She would stand condemned by all but a few (like Dolores), repudiated and punished by them, not by him. In destroying himself he destroyed her, destroyed the bond that chained him to his guilt, destroyed everyone who was linked to that guilt. Those who had gone unpunished for his loss would be castigated by his self-punishing death.

But even now he could not leave undone the tasks that remained to be done; no one should say of him that at the end he had failed what was due. And in these last, deliberate acts of delivering the calf, delivering the señorita's share of the money, ensuring Ana fetched the calf back when ordered to, is reflected the full intent of his final act: absolute order for the rupture of order to be absolute. His suicide, I believe, then, was intended to be understood precisely as the deliberate summation of what was his due.

In the grey light of the parlour behind the closed door he laid the money carefully on the mahogany table and stepped back, head bowed, for her to count and return his share of the notes. There was a silence of which he was unaware: she was looking and unforgivingly seeing his brother in him.

'You've miscounted, Miguel.' The voice was quiet, had an edge. 'You've shortchanged yourself.'

'Eh?' His head rose slowly. He stammered something that

was meant as an excuse, in the torment of guilt he sensed a new cause of threat: the exposure of insufficiency at its most determinedly masked point, the reputation built up over years of hard work: an irreproachable man in every aspect of work. His head hung again, knowing his guilt: the deal was bad, should never have been made ...

'Shortchange yourself if you want, but you won't shortchange me.'

And then it began. With the self-righteous anger of those whose right is to command, whose right is embodied in the property they own, she lashed at this man, whose only right was to labour and make her a profit from her land. What right had he to sell Tío Bigote the calf cheap? What right to sell what was hers because he wanted to buy Tío Bigote's land? What right to listen to that foreigner's words, to think he could benefit from their dam? What right, what right?

None. She saw his eyes staring hollowly like a dumb animal's and the pain incensed her to a fury she wouldn't try to contain. A sharecropper who existed only thanks to her, to whom she had kept her promise made when he was a child, who had the effrontery to think that he could leave her at will to buy his own land ... For the first and only time she flung at him the scene in the cowshed when, as a small boy, she had warned him of his future as he cowered in her grasp. And he, what had he done? Paid no heed to her words, taken advantage of her because she was a woman defenceless in this world of men. Worse, he'd betrayed his own father for his brother's ways, believing that he had the right to the land he worked. Such arrogance, like his brother's, must and would be cut down.

Never before had she such cause for unleashing her woman's and landlord's revenge, and her anger reached out for the words that destroy.

Hearing, he heard nothing but his confirmed guilt. *Scoundrel!*

She screamed again and again, and his eyes were frenzied with the desire to escape, to negate the destruction by destroying himself, as he stood there without moving, incapable of reflex. Without shame, without honour, all maleness destroyed, the void torn apart by the truth of disgrace, vomiting out the bloodied offence ...

'Take these,' she threw the notes at his feet, 'take them and fetch the calf back. Now get out.'

He stumbled into the street. There was nothing left. Friends called him for coffee and he went by without answering, his face deathly pale. Before him he saw the open shop. Guilt and recrimination fled into a frozen calm, and he waited in the doorway until the few customers left. His mind had cleared, the pain was gone. Testing the rope between his arms he smiled. Neither doubt nor hesitation imperilled his will. A few yards from the shop he stopped in front of Juana's house. The door was shut, he didn't knock. He was free, dependent on no one, self-sufficient at last. There would be no failure. He smiled again: with pride, with honour, without disgrace.

46

Closures

John stared out of the window at the rain. Below, a man half ran beneath a piece of sacking uselessly held over his head. With each step his feet disappeared under the water, which foamed round his ankles; the street was a torrent.

Drained, totally consumed by the account of Miguel's last hours, John was only slowly beginning to return to himself. As his sense of autonomy revived it was accompanied by a deep grief; for the first time, he mourned his friend.

There was anger in his mourning, too. Miguel had gone to his self-inflicted death with pride and honour, self-sufficient at last. Or so it had seemed to John. The failures of Juana, María Burgos and of himself were indisputable; but the values for which, in this account, Miguel had died did not seem to merit such sacrifice. Miguel could well still be alive, he thought angrily. But after a time his anger had slackened and he was overcome by sadness. It made no more sense to condemn Miguel for his values than to blame him for having lived in this society.

Mourning for a friend he still believed he could have saved, he felt Miguel as a part of him now. He would never outlive that sense of guilt; but it no longer dominated because, deep in him, Miguel lived on – standing in the middle of the terrace, the centre of his world, watching the soil turn dark as the water flowed slowly along the furrow. A passion ...

This inner image of Miguel John owed to his obsession. Originating in guilt, the obsession had changed course during the writing. From being an attempt to understand Miguel, it had become a passion to explore whether he could convincingly bring him to life on paper. Could John persuade a mythical reader (he thought now of Dave), apprised of the same few facts as himself, that this was how Miguel's life might have been? A fiction. But when all was said and done, was it possible to understand another person totally? Weren't even those closest to us an on-going invention sustained by our own subjective perceptions? Wasn't each of us invented by the other – and probably in as great a measure by ourselves?

Smiling, he recalled Genet's rejection of Sartre's 'saintly', voluminous exegesis of him, and wondered which of the two was closer to the truth: subject or author. The subject, of course, he was tempted to say, in good common sense. But did it not make equally good sense to refuse a person's self-characterization as the sole criterion of character? Couldn't imagination, well focused and empathetic, come closer to reality than a subject's own view of himself? Closer, also, than a compilation of biographical facts? Perhaps then, as he'd always wanted to believe, the novel was the privileged site of understanding the being of others.

If this were so, he had been slow to recognize that seeing the world through Miguel's eyes had provided a new focus on his own life. His deep-rooted *indifference* had emerged more clearly in writing about Miguel than in any of the pages he'd devoted to writing about himself. This deeply paralysing sense of uselessness, this inner vacuum, which brought with it the impossibility of believing that his acts mattered to anyone, was the fundamental flaw he'd been searching for. It had been there all the while in front of his eyes and he'd refused to recognize it. But as he relived his relationship with Miguel and Bob, with Dolores too, he'd been made aware of its recurring pattern, which expressed itself in his passive role; yet this passivity was also a form of activity, allowing him to shrug off others' problems in the knowledge that what he, John, did made not a ha'penny worth of difference in the real world.

He got up and put the folder with Miguel's story into the half-packed suitcase, on top of the pages of self-examination. He would never need to return to either again. On the floor under the window the pool of water was growing wider; water dripped from the bedroom ceiling; everything was damp. Now it remained only to act on his new-found awareness, he thought, as he went to the wardrobe to fetch his few clothes and put them in the suitcase. It was a gesture, no more, because his intended departure, already postponed by the rain, appeared no more imminent than it had for the past several days. The village's charcoal-burning taxi was held up by flooding in Torre del Mar. Over the mountains, Dolores had heard on the radio, a flash flood had swept two people to their deaths when a bridge collapsed.

Revelling in the rain, the sound of water cascading down the village streets and pouring off onto the land, he had at the beginning gone out every day. The fury of this unexpected onslaught excited him. New ravines opened in the earth to take the flow, the watercourses were churning with mud-coloured water. From a distance, he saw the water tumbling down Bob's watercourse and he imagined the dam filling in the depths of the gorge; it brought with it an ambivalent sense of satisfaction. Perhaps, after all, to store some of this immense, wasted fall would bring benefits to those other sharecroppers who would need it next year.

But he hadn't ventured down the track to the gorge. Now

that he had finished writing about Miguel, he knew that his relationship with Benalamar was at an end. This land was a vice for people like him who needed suffering and harshness to feel themselves come alive. To try to become one with it was a form of escapism, a vicarious way of not being, as the attempt to write about Miguel had finally demonstrated to him.

Preferring the downpour to the sodden atmosphere of the house, he decided now to go out. From the doorway he saw that the top part of the village was lost in cloud while in front of him the rain fell perpendicular on the watery street. In a few steps from his house he was soaked through. The square was under several feet of water and people had piled what they could in front of their doors to keep out the flood.

Skirting the square, he went down the street that led to the start of the track. From the threshing floor he saw that a giant boulder had been dislodged by the rain and crashed over several terraces below, uprooting a large carob tree in its fall. The land was riven with fissures cut by the rushing water, which carried with it great quantities of topsoil, leaving behind it a litter of stones.

In the distance he heard a booming noise that could only be water, and thought he saw people on the track by the gap in the hills. He wiped the water out of his eyes. No, it was too far to see clearly enough through the rain. The booming grew louder, coming definitely from below, and suddenly he knew what it was and began to run, slipping and stumbling down the track. But before he had gone more than half way, an enormous series of crashes, like hundreds of boulders being torn from their bearings, thundered in the air, followed instantly by a tidal roar. 'Oh God!' he moaned and slipped to the ground.

Before his eyes the land below the hills seemed to vanish as the water burst from the dam, unfurling for a moment in a slow-motion wave before it caught the momentum of its own weight. Behind the white crest the water rushed on, almost indistinguishable in colour from the earth. Now he saw clearly that people were running through the gap in the hills, and he thought he could hear their cries. In a moment he was on his feet and stumbling again down the track in the near-blinding rain.

In the gap, he caught sight of several faces he knew but couldn't name, who shouted incomprehensibly at him. He ran on until he came out on the track above the gorge. It was immediately apparent what had happened: the top third of the stone wall, which lacked the protection of the unfinished concrete wall, had given way under the weight of water, which had backed up to the top. There were no conduits to channel it away. One part of the stone wall hung like a broken arm, a stream of water still flowing round it, while the other had crashed and disappeared into the water below.

Fearfully, John looked down beyond the wall. Matanzas and El Vicente were still standing, he saw, but ... He wiped the rain from his face, disbelieving: was that roofless broken shell surrounded by water all that remained of El Mayorazgo? In a panic he started to run. Casa Colorada had vanished, he saw as he rounded the corner and almost fell over Ana.

Huddled on the track she was weeping, a tangle of wet hair over her face. He knelt beside her. 'What happened, what happened?' he asked pointlessly.

'Mother!' she sobbed. 'Mother!'

'Where is she? Tell me.'

'Mother!'

'Was she in the house?'

All he heard were her sobs; she didn't reply. He got up and ran on. Soon he was wading through water up to his knees, his thighs, then his chest. He reached the shattered cottage and struggled to find a way in, for the roof had collapsed on top of the doorway. At last he pushed his way in through a broken wall and saw the devastation. The wall, which had taken the main brunt, had collapsed and the shattered remains of chairs, beds, cooking utensils, floated in the water; the tintype of the blonde hung incongruously from a twisted rafter.

'Señora!' he shouted. 'Señora!'

For a moment he thought of diving below the surface to look for her; but the water was like liquid earth and he could see nothing. He pushed his way out through the ruptured wall.

'Señora!' The shout echoed emptily over the water, over the uprooted trees. Near the house, one of the cows was belly-up in the water and a bit farther off the calf floated entwined in the branches of an almond. Only the carob was still standing, he observed, and that was when he saw her, crumpled like a black rag doll, in the bottom branches. Christ! He waded across, believing that she was still alive, but when he got close he saw by her contorted face that she was dead. She looked as though she were shouting with anger and one arm was pointing with fingers outstretched.

Hesitantly, he put a hand out; she was the first dead person he had touched. Gathering up courage he lifted her down by the armpits, surprised at how little she weighed. Then he slung her over his shoulder and waded towards the rising land from which he'd come. He was unsure whether he ought to be moving her because almost certainly he was infringing some law governing corpses, but he thought he would argue that one out later. Now and again her body seemed to twitch and, scared, he wanted to drop her; but he knew he had committed himself to getting her out and tried to ignore these frightening spasms. She was dead after all, he reassured himself.

When he reached the place where he had left Ana, she was no longer there. He walked on. It was still raining torrentially. If there was no one in the gap in the hills he'd leave the corpse there and walk back to the village to inform the Guardia Civil.

In the gap, however, he found a group of men sheltering under the giant boulder. He laid the body down gently before them. He didn't see that Ana was crouched among them; but she saw him and the burden he was carrying, and she rushed at him screaming. Before he knew what was happening she hit him across the face several times, and it was only the intervention of one of the men that ended her assault.

'Assassin!' she shouted, slumping on the ground.

'He's not to blame,' said the man, whom John recognized as Culebra. 'It's the other. I foresaw this happening. That wall was never safe.'

'My mother, God rest her soul, knew that,' Ana cried. 'Didn't she get the building stopped! Miguel told her the wall wouldn't hold.'

John looked at her, at the men. He knew, they all could have known, that but for the dead woman's determination to stop the building, the dam's inner retaining wall could have been finished before the rains came. The top part of the dam had burst only because the stone wall remained unprotected by concrete.

'We knew early this morning it was going to burst,' said Culebra, 'because we saw the wall bulging. We warned everyone. Only she wouldn't leave.'

'But why?' John expostulated. 'She was the one who said it was dangerous.'

'The dam and the señorita had taken her son's life, let them take hers, that's what she said. Ana begged her on her knees to leave, and only just escaped herself. But she wouldn't come. From up here we saw her walking round and round the house, then she started to make for the dam, shouting words we couldn't make out. It was then that it burst and she disappeared under the water. I think she went mad, what with Miguel, and having to leave the farm.'

'Leave?'

'Yes, now that there isn't a man to work the land. The señorita came down last week to tell her.'

'I see,' replied John. 'Well, there's her body. I'm leaving it with you. I'll inform the Guardia Civil when I get to the village. You'll have to take care of the rest.' He wiped away the sweat on his face and started the climb back to the village.

That evening the total exhaustion returned and he collapsed, shivering with cold. Dolores wrapped him in blankets she warmed by the stove and brought him steaming cups of broth. His head lost its moorings and for a time he was delirious. Dolores feared pneumonia and called in the doctor who, to her relief, could find nothing wrong. By noon the next day he was better; and when in the afternoon he heard the church bell tolling he got up, despite Dolores's protestations, and went out.

The heavy rain had turned to a drizzle and the cloud had lifted from the top of the village. On the threshing floor, as he expected, a number of men were gathered waiting. From there, the damage done by the dam's flood waters was hidden by the hills; but the rain's work was visible everywhere else in terrace walls that had collapsed, in uprooted trees and boulders strewn over the countryside. The land had been scoured by the rain. It was the heaviest rainfall in living memory, he overheard one of the men say.

'Ay! It'll be months before the land is fit to sow,' said another.

'Months! It'll be a year before El Mayorazgo and Casa Colorada can be ploughed. Tío Bigote was lucky to have sold.'

'It's the Englishman's problem now,' said the first.

'He went away just in time, perhaps he won't want to be coming back,' laughed a young man.

'Don't be stupid. He'll only have paid the ten per cent deposit. He might rather lose it than pay for land that's destroyed,' replied another.

'And El Mayorazgo? The señorita needn't have thrown them out, eh?'

'Ay! First Miguel, then his mother. Who'd sharecrop for her?' said the first.

'There's plenty would. But the land is lost now. Miguel always said the wall wouldn't hold.'

'Poor man! It's a good thing he didn't live to see this.'

John was expecting these comments. But the earlier phrases had left him bewildered. 'Did you say Tío Bigote was selling his farm?'

'What's left of it now, that's right, to your compatriot, they say.'

'But!' Out of the corner of his eye, he noticed Tío Bigote on the far side of the threshing floor. He went across and stood next to him. After a decent interval, he asked the old man politely if what he had heard were true.

'Look here, señor, fifty-five years I've worked the land and now I can retire, thanks to a foreigner. And what do I see? The land it took my father seven years to pay off, making charcoal, threshing, borrowing from the señorita's father – the land is gone, ruined.'

'But it is not your land any more, is that correct?'

'Yes, that is correct. But who tilled and fertilized that land? Who dug the terraces? Who planted the trees and built the house? The land is more than a piece of paper, more than money ...'

'Yes.'

The time had come, John thought, to put the question at last. The old man's lined face seemed to tighten suddenly. 'Miguel? Eh, he mentioned it once. But he wasn't serious about it, couldn't be.' There was a long pause as he looked at the hills where a car could be seen climbing the road. It was coming too fast to be the taxi. A foreigner's car, defying the rain, almost certainly. Then the old man turned: 'With the dam it was worth more than anyone here could pay. Miguel knew that, it was why he didn't insist. And now thanks to the dam, that land is a ruin.'

There was a stir among the men as they moved to the edge of the threshing floor. John looked down: the pine hill, the rushing watercourse, the familiar, rain-washed track. And then, far below through the gap in the hills, Miguel's mother's coffin appeared.